There had been hunger in his gaze

Carefully, quietly, she rolled onto her back, then turned her head just enough so that she could glimpse his profile in the darkness.

There'd also been disdain. And curiosity. And desire.

Damn the man.

Damn all men, for that matter.

Sleep, she counseled herself. Sleep and forget them.

She sighed, rolled over and punched her pillow. The train whooshed into another tunnel, rattling the windows and making her ears pop. Tom whimpered softly in his sleep. MacPherson snored.

It was going to be a very long night.

ANNE McALLISTER was born in California. She spent long lazy summers daydreaming on local beaches and studying surfers, swimmers and volleyball players in an effort to find the perfect hero. She finally did, not on the beach, but in a university library where she was working. She, her husband and their four children have since moved to the Midwest. She taught, copyedited, capped deodorant bottles and ghostwrote sermons before turning to her first love, writing romance fiction.

Books by Anne McAllister

HARLEQUIN PRESENTS

844—LIGHTNING STORM
1060—TO TAME A WOLF
1099—THE MARRIAGE TRAP
1257—ONCE A HERO
1371—OUT OF BOUNDS
1459—ISLAND INTERLUDE
1620—CALL UP THE WIND

HARLEQUIN AMERICAN ROMANCE

309—SAVING GRACE
341—IMAGINE
387—I THEE WED
459—MACKENZIE'S BABY
466—A COWBOY FOR CHRISTMAS

Anne McAllister

Catch Me If You Can

Harlequin Books

TORONTO • NEW YORK • LONDON
AMSTERDAM • PARIS • SYDNEY • HAMBURG
STOCKHOLM • ATHENS • TOKYO • MILAN
MADRID • WARSAW • BUDAPEST • AUCKLAND

For Tom, Julie and Allison
And for Donald and Christa

ISBN 0-373-11680-2

CATCH ME IF YOU CAN

This edition published by arrangement with Harlequin Enterprises B. V.

Printed in U.S.A.

CHAPTER ONE

"THE important thing," Emily said as she flung clothes into her duffel bag and scrabbled under the bed for her shoes, "is not to panic."

Her neighbor Gloria watched, leaning back against the headboard, sipping a soft drink complacently in the midst of the whirlwind. "Right," she drawled. "You're right, of course."

"I mean," Emily went on, stuffing her feet into her espadrilles and zipping up the bag, "given the commitments of the great Alejandro, chances are he won't even bother to look for us."

"Of course," Gloria said between sips.

Emily raked a comb distractedly through her long ash blond hair. "But I'm not going to sit here in case he does. Not in Barcelona. It'd be different if we were in the States. That's my home base, not his. But here—oh, no. Alejandro Gomez probably knows every competent lawyer in Spain. He probably *owns* every competent lawyer in Spain. He'd have Tom away from me in a minute."

Gloria wisely refrained from agreeing with that.

She only smiled sadly and sympathized with her friend's dilemma. They'd only known each other for the past year, ever since Emily had come to stay in her sister-in-law's apartment and met Gloria who lived downstairs. But, despite their relatively short acquaintance, they'd become close.

Gloria, an expatriate artist, had supported Emily through the months of her sister-in-law's illness and eventual death. She'd been there for Emily to lean on when she'd had no one else. She'd taken care of Emily's six-year-old nephew Tom after school while Emily had given language lessons, insisting that Emily needed to get out and do something other than hover around her nephew.

She'd even tried to get Emily to date, telling her that life had to go on. But, though Emily agreed with the sentiment, there were limits.

She didn't want to date. Not after her disastrous engagement to Marc.

Emily's fast-lane life as a top-flight Paris model had assured her the company of more men over the past five years than she'd believed possible when she'd been growing up in the American midwest.

At first, charmed by their interest, she'd taken them all at face value, naively believing they liked her as a person, not simply as a beautiful face.

"Such innocence. You have such innocence," her friend, photographer Howell Evans, was always telling her. "That's the beauty of you."

But Emily didn't realize how innocent she really was until she met Marc Fontenot.

The handsome young car manufacturer had introduced himself at a Monte Carlo party, monopolized her evening, begun haunting her shows, her shoots, her life.

Everywhere she went, she'd found Marc already there, strong, virile, witty and enchanting, so cleverly charming that he swept her off her feet before she knew it. Worldly, debonair Marc was the antithesis of the men she'd grown up with. And Emily had been unsophisticated enough to think she'd charmed him, to think that he'd fallen in love with her just as she'd fallen in love with him.

When he'd asked her to marry him, she'd jumped to say yes.

If she hadn't overheard that phone call with his mistress the night before the wedding, she might have been married to him now. Thank heavens she had, picking up the phone and to hear him tell Lisette that he didn't really care about the woman he was to marry in what was to be one of Paris's most publicized weddings. "Don't worry, *chérie*, you are my own true love," he'd said softly. "Emily, she is for show. Goes with the image. She looks good on paper, you know?"

Devastated, Emily hadn't waited around to discuss matters with him. Instead she'd run, making a thoughtless, panicky midnight dash to Howell's apartment.

The paparazzi, expecting a sunny April wedding and getting instead a perplexed and furious jilted bridegroom, had had a field day with her defection.

But the one who had spotted her driving out of Paris in Howell's Jaguar had got the biggest scoop of all.

Grainy black and white photos and two-inch headlines proclaiming Emily's infidelity to Marc and Howell's to his famous reclusive sculptress wife had been everywhere before the week was out.

Emily had been frantic.

"Don't worry about it," Howell, ever complacent, had told her.

But she had. She'd hated the notoriety, the falsehoods, the lunacy of it all. It was phony, foolish and wrongheaded, and she'd wanted to make it right again.

"I'll talk to the Press, tell them," she'd said to Howell.

But he had simply laughed and shaken his head. "The damage—what little there is—has already been done, Emily. You'll only make it worse by talking about it. Haven't you ever heard about women who protest too much?"

Emily had, but she was still uncomfortable with it. The curious looks, the snickers, the silences when she came into a room. It unnerved her.

Marielena's phone call, awful as it was, had come as a sort of salvation.

In nursing Mari and in caring for Tom, Emily had got her balance again. She realized how much she hated the crazy life-style she'd been living, how she wanted a plain, simple life.

She had been trying to get it in the months since Mari's death. She'd thought she'd been making progress for both herself and for Tom.

And now this!

"Ready?" Gloria asked now.

Emily glanced at her watch, bit her lip, then hefted her bag. She felt even more nervous than she was letting on. Cloak-and-dagger was not her style.

But ever since the head of Tom's school had told her of the letter they'd received from Alejandro Gomez, her late sister-in-law's high-powered brother, advising them to direct all bills and correspondence about Tom's education to him, she'd been worrying.

Marielena had never had anything to do with her family since she'd married Emily's brother, David, seven years before. The Gomezes hadn't approved. They hadn't come to the wedding. They hadn't been at Tom's baptism. They'd washed their hands of Marielena, and she of them. She hadn't even got back in touch with them after David died when his navy plane went down in the Mediterranean three years before. Nor had she contacted them when she'd become ill.

"No," she'd said adamantly when Emily had suggested calling them. "They didn't want me when I married David. Now I don't want them!"

"But what about... about Tom?"

"When I am gone, Tom will be yours. You love him."

Emily did. More than anything or anyone in the world.

Tom was all the family she had. Her father had died when she was fifteen and her mother three years later. David had been her only sibling.

"You will do the best for him. I know that." Mari's dark eyes had fixed on her confidently.

"Of course I will," Emily had promised, but she'd heard plenty about the greedy, tough-minded patriarch of the Gomez family. "But won't they try to take him away?"

Marielena's features had clouded. "Never! They had their chance. They didn't want us when I was alive. They will not get Tom when I am dead."

After the first couple of months, when no word had come from Mari's family, Emily had breathed more easily, thinking that all was well.

When she discovered, quite by accident, reading a business weekly over the shoulder of a fellow subway rider, that Alfredo Gomez y Ramirez had died of a heart attack only a few weeks after Mari's death, she had breathed more easily still. It was the father she'd feared. But now it appeared she had been wrong.

"Send the bills to him? Ridiculous. I'm Tom's guardian," Emily had protested to the secretary at her nephew's school.

The woman had smiled indulgently. "Ah, *sí*, *señorita*, of course you are. But Señor Gomez is a very important man. *Muy rico*, *no*?"

Very rich, yes. And very powerful—more so since his father's death. And suddenly obviously very interested in his nephew.

Emily shivered at the thought.

"He says his nephew is his responsibility," the secretary went on.

Emily shook her head. "He's mine."

But she knew that her assertion wouldn't mean much if Gomez decided to press the issue. Alejandro Gomez had far more influence in Spain than she did.

"A Gomez can do anything he wants," Mari had told her once.

"He couldn't stop you marrying David," Emily had reminded her.

"Because I am a Gomez, too!"

Well, Emily wasn't a Gomez and didn't want to be. But if Alejandro Gomez thought he was going to take her nephew, he was wrong.

"I'm ready," she said to Gloria. "If Tom and I are going to be on that train, it's time to go."

"Do you think Gomez is watching the building?" Gloria asked.

A week ago Emily would have laughed at the notion. But that was before Tom had said a strange man tried to talk to him on the playground, before a letter had come from Gomez's solicitor, before the great man himself had had his secretary call her on the phone.

"Señor Gomez will be pleased to take his nephew for the summer holidays," she had told Emily in a haughty tone.

"Señor Gomez," Emily had replied frostily, "will please leave his nephew alone."

There was a moment's silence on the other end of the line. Then the woman had said, "Now see here, *señorita*. Señor Gomez is a very powerful man. You would do well to pay attention to him."

"I don't have to pay attention to him," Emily had said just as firmly.

"His nephew——"

"His nephew is also my nephew. And I have custody of him," Emily retorted.

It was debatable which of them had hung up first.

Later that day there had been a ring at the doorbell for their apartment. "I'll get it," Tom had said, scrambling to his feet.

"No! I mean, I don't want you to answer it," Emily had said, carefully modulating her voice, aware of the intensity of her first panicked reaction.

Tom looked puzzled. "How come?"

"Salesmen," Emily had fabricated. "You know what pests they can be."

Of course Tom didn't. And Emily had no idea if there were really door-to-door salesmen in Barcelona anyway. She just didn't want Tom answering the door. She had been all too sure who it would be.

"What if somebdoy else lets him in?"

A helpful neighbor, leaving the building, sometimes simply held the door open for whoever was ringing the bell.

"Then we just won't answer it up here," Emily had said. "But I doubt that will happen. See?" she'd said after a few moments' quiet. "He's gone."

But he hadn't, as the almost immediate pounding on the door so clearly proved.

"Wow," Tom had breathed, his eyes round. "I wonder what he's selling."

Emily had grimaced. She'd tugged Tom into the kitchen. "Come on. Let's get started on supper. He'll go away."

But it had taken fifteen minutes of intermittent pounding before he did. And the event had left Emily shaking so much that as soon as she put Tom to bed that night she began to make plans.

She didn't want to disrupt Tom's school year, but it was almost over anyway. And one of the virtues of Mari's insistence on his attending one of the American schools in Barcelona was that it operated on the same schedule as American schools did. Consequently he'd only miss a few days if she took him out now in the middle of June.

And after the door-pounding incident, she had made up her mind to take him out. Not only out of school, but out of Spain.

However legal her guardianship might be, she had no faith in her ability to defend her right to her nephew in the face of the clout wielded by one of the most influential men in the whole country—a man who had family connections and business interests everywhere.

"Why not fly to the States right away?" Gloria wanted to know now.

"That's what he'd expect. He'd stop me for sure."

"What if he finds out about this? What if he follows you?"

"I can fade into the woodwork as well as anyone."

"With your face?"

"It's been a year since I was plastered on every subway wall in that perfume ad. And the photos from the fiasco with Marc were so bad no one would recognize me."

Gloria didn't look convinced. She surveyed Emily's long ash blond hair and wide green eyes, her full lips and delicately molded cheekbones. "Even so..."

"Trust me."

"Well..." Gloria brightened "...if you see him, you can run the other way."

"I don't know what he looks like."

Gloria was shocked. "You haven't even seen a picture?"

"Marielena wouldn't have any in the house. 'They're dead to me,' she used to say."

"But a man so well-known, wouldn't he be in the magazines?"

"Not the great Alejandro. He keeps a very low profile. I've looked, believe me, but I've never found one. I've seen exactly one of his father—in the obituary. He had slick dark hair and a sinister moustache just like a bad guy in an old western." Emily wrinkled her nose. "No doubt the son is much the same."

"Is he married?"

"I don't know. He wasn't the last I heard. Unlike Marc, he doesn't seem to go for articles or photos. Or publicity of any kind. Not of the personal variety in any case. I can find out anything I want to know about the companies the family owns, but nothing at all about the family itself."

"Didn't Mari say anything?"

Emily shook her head. "Never. It was as if they'd ceased to exist for her."

"Maybe she didn't care."

"I think she cared too much. I think their disapproval hurt her so much she just wouldn't talk about them at all." Emily recalled the number of times she'd tried to bring up the topic of her sister-in-law's family, only to have Mari become agitated and change the subject. "I can't believe that any family could be so cruel, but apparently they were." She sighed and opened the front door. "Come on. Let's get going."

"Are you picking Tom up at school?"

"Bob Duggan's bringing him to the station."

Gloria's brows lifted at that. "I'll bet Bob was pleased."

"He's a friend," Emily said firmly.

Bob Duggan was the teacher at Tom's school whom she had gone around with now and then. Emily suspected he wanted rather more than that, but she didn't. And that was that, as far as she was concerned.

She hadn't wanted to drag him into this business with Gomez at all, knowing he might get the wrong idea, but she didn't have any other choice.

"Does Tom know about the trip?"

"I told him last night. Not why. Marielena never talked to him about her family, and I certainly didn't want to bring up anything that might make him think there was some big bad uncle who might snatch him away. He's had enough trauma for one little boy. I just said we were going on holiday."

"So if not the States, where?"

Emily reached for her bag. "Can't tell you. If you don't know, the big bad uncle won't be able to get it out of you."

Gloria laughed. "You're crazy. I hardly think he's going to torture me to find you."

Emily hoped not. She hoped he'd forget the whole thing. In her more rational moments, she thought he might.

A man with multinational business interests like Alejandro Gomez would surely have plenty of more important things to keep him busy than a nephew he'd never seen. He might be interested right now, but if she could just get away and stay away for a few weeks she was fairly confident he'd forget all about her—and Tom.

"Here." She handed the suitcase to Gloria. "If he is lurking out there, I want him to think it's you going on the trip. I'm just coming down to see you off. Then we'll take separate taxis."

Gloria looked impressed. "Very clever."

"Very desperate," Emily corrected. She shut off the light, steered her friend out of the apartment and didn't look back.

Gloria, with Emily's duffel, had already arrived at the train station by the time Emily did.

Emily found her at once. But in the bustle and rumble of thousands of travelers she began to fear that she and Bob might not even connect. He was the only one she'd confided her immediate destination to. And that was because it was the only way to ensure that they'd meet at the right train.

"Sure you don't want me to come with you?" Gloria asked as Emily took her duffel.

"Thanks, but I'll go on alone. Open any mail you think is important. Water the plants. I'll call when I can."

She gave Gloria a quick hug, then walked away quickly toward the board with the departure schedule, found the destination she was looking for, descended the escalator, and almost sagged with relief to find Tom waiting with Bob at the bottom.

Bob hurried toward her. Tom was hopping from one foot to the other, a gleam of anticipation in his eye, a delighted grin on his face. It made her aware of how seldom she'd seen him smile since Mari's death, and how far she had to go to bring the happy-go-lucky nephew she remembered back to being himself again.

"This is it, Em. This is our train!" He was certainly eager enough right now.

She turned to Bob. "Did you find the right car?"

"Right back there. Two seats reserved for Cerbère." He reached for her, taking her arm possessively, and Emily wondered if she'd done the right thing in involving him.

She cleared her throat nervously. "Is there anyone else in the compartment?"

"No. But there's one more seat reserved besides yours."

Emily's fingers tightened around the handle of her bag and she looked around nervously. But besides a Pakistani family, a couple of harried-looking businessmen and an old lady with a shopping bag, she didn't see anyone boarding the train.

"Do you think you were followed?" she asked Bob quietly, hoping that Tom, hunkered down and staring under the railway carriage, wouldn't hear.

"Not that I could see." He smiled and touched her hair. "You should have been a spy, Em. I think you're home free."

She pulled away slightly, then sighed. "I don't think I'll be home free until I get back to the States."

"When will that be?"

She grimaced. "When Uncle Dearest has lost interest. It won't take long—I hope." Emily crossed her fingers.

"I'll be going back to Boston as soon as school is over. I can call you——"

She shook her head. "I don't know where I'll be."

"When you find out, call me." He scribbled an address and thrust it at her. Emily took it and stuffed it in her bag. She wouldn't call. There was no reason for her to think that she could pursue a friendship with Bob when he had other ideas. It wouldn't be fair, and Emily really didn't want to lead him on.

He slipped an arm around her shoulders. "Are you sure you have to do this?"

Emily looked down at Tom's dark head, at the sturdy body and small stubborn chin that so reminded her of David's. Her throat tightened whenever she contemplated the possibility that he might be taken from her, that she might never see him again. "What else could I possibly do?" she asked with quiet anguish.

"You could marry me."

She took an involuntary step backward, her eyes widening.

Bob lifted his chin, looking defiant now. "Why not? A single woman has far less chance of keeping custody than a married one."

"I don't think——"

"You know I care for you."

"Well, I——"

He raked a hand through his fair hair. "I know we've never discussed marriage..."

They'd never even come close, Emily thought, staring at him as if he'd grown another head.

"But you must know how I feel. And, given the circumstances, you really ought to think about it."

Emily felt her cheeks burn. Her mouth opened. "Bob, I like you. Truly I do. But I don't think——"

"Don't think—yet." He reached out a finger and gently closed her mouth. "But keep it in the back of your mind, Emily, just in case." He gave her a rueful look. "I love you. And even if you don't feel the same way, you have to admit it could be a good idea—for Tom. And——" his mouth crooked into a hopeful grin "—I think you might learn to love me."

Emily's fingers twisted together. Love? She wasn't even sure what the word meant. Not after Marc.

But she appreciated the gesture, even as she knew she couldn't take advantage of it.

She reached out and briefly touched his cheek, wanting to thank him and at the same time say she could never consider it. The thought of Alejandro Gomez stopped her.

What if he really did try to take Tom away from her?

Could she say outright that she would never consider marrying to keep custody of her nephew? In a normal, sane world, of course she never would marry a man she didn't love. But if it was the only way she could be sure to give Tom the life he deserved?

She dropped her hand. Her eyes mets Bob's. "Thank you. You are very kind."

"It's not kindness, Emily."

Tom tugged her hand. "Come on, Em. It's time." He pointed to his watch importantly, then towed her the toward steps. "See you, Mr. Duggan."

Bob's smile was wry. "See you, Tom." His gaze shifted to meet Emily's. "I mean it," he told her. "I will see you. Even if you don't come back here."

He leaned toward her, caught her in his arms and gave her a hug that was neither reassuring nor quick. Then he kissed her hard and stepped back. "You don't have to think about marriage right now," he said. "You can, however, think about that."

Emily, dazed from the ferocity of his kiss, stumbled up the steps into the car, mind reeling, lips trembling. "A favor," she muttered. "I only wanted a favor."

"Huh?" Tom peered up at her, confused.

"Nothing, dear." She gave him a shaky grin, then peered at the seat reservations, then at the tickets stuck in the wall of the compartment.

"Here we are," she said brightly even as she felt another twinge of apprehension seeing the third seat reservation tucked in the pocket. The way her life had been going lately...

She opened the door, half ready to bolt.

Sitting next to the window was a nun.

The sister, eighty if she was a day, nodded and patted the seat next to her, beckoning to Tom. She said something to him in Spanish which Emily, not yet fully fluent, wasn't able to catch. But Tom nodded happily and bounced onto the seat beside her, chattering in his mother's native tongue.

Emily wrestled their duffels on to the luggage rack overhead, all the while listening to him talk, catching the drift, aware that he was telling the sister that they were off on holiday, that he didn't have to go back to school at all until autumn, that he was going to have a super time. He sounded as cheerful as she'd heard him in months.

His mother's death had devastated him, even though she knew he had sensed it was inevitable. He had borne it stoically for the most part, only sobbing at night until Emily came to comfort him. Recently she thought he'd been sleeping much better, adjusting to life with her, to the family being just the two of them. She looked down at his dark head now, listened to his eager voice and ached with love for this small boy who had known so much loss in his life.

She was determined he wouldn't lose her as well.

Before she settled into the seat, she checked back out into the corridor. The only voices she heard were those of a pair of American schoolteachers discussing budgetary cutbacks and puffing cigarettes. Not a high-powered Spaniard in sight. For the first time in days Emily breathed more easily.

In a few short hours they would be in France. By morning they would arrive in Switzerland. Guido Farantino, another of her photographer friends, had a house there. She hadn't called to say she was coming. But he and Sophie, his wife, had given her a standing invitation. They wouldn't be expecting her to bring a child, but she knew he wouldn't care.

In any case, she didn't think she'd have to impose on them for long. Every day or so she'd check with Gloria to try to determine if Alejandro Gomez had given up looking for them.

Not *if*, she told herself. When.

He would. She was sure he would.

Pressing her lips together, crossing her fingers, she shut the door again and settled back into the seat next to Tom.

They had to change trains at Cerbère, leaving the RENFE coach train behind and heading toward Passport Control before they could board the sleeper car that would take them through France during the night and deposit them bright and early the next morning in Geneva.

"We get to sleep on the train?" Tom was clearly delighted with the news. "In beds?"

"Couchettes," Emily told him. "Bunk beds, really."

"I always wanted bunk beds. And on a train! Where is it?" Tom was hopping up and down trying to catch a glimpse of the train.

"Through there." Emily nodded toward the door through which they would pass after they got through Passport Control.

The door, to Tom, meant a train with bunks. To Emily, it meant freedom from the long arm of Alejandro Gomez.

Once through it she would be in France. Safe.

She glanced around nervously now, half expecting a huge, intimidating Alejandro Gomez to loom up out of nowhere and bar her way.

She and Tom were being jostled along in a multinational sea of travelers, mostly university students, grubby and unshaven, but clearly having the time of their lives. Here and there she saw families, a few solitary travelers with packs on their backs, businessmen with black briefcases and tan raincoats.

"'Sa matter?" Tom asked her.

"Nothing." She gave him a bright smile, then glanced behind her again, one more time. For luck, she told herself.

And there he was!

She didn't need a picture. It was all too obvious. It could be no one else. Just descending the train, obviously in a hurry, pushing past people, a determined dark-haired man was striding in her direction.

He was a younger version of the picture she'd seen of Alfredo, right down to the slicked back hair and pencil-thin moustache.

Desperately she looked for an escape, stumbled into a couple carrying a baby and apologized in three languages.

"Are you okay?" Tom asked.

"F-fine. I——" She watched enviously as the man in the couple took the baby from his wife, then helped her adjust her pack. She wished she had someone to share her burden.

She wished fleetingly that Bob had come. If she had Bob along she might have had a chance. She supposed it was too much to hope that Gomez didn't know what she and Tom looked like. But if only for a moment he thought she was with Bob, thought she was married, that Tom was her child, it might give him pause to reconsider; it might be enough.

And even though Bob wasn't here...

She grabbed Tom's hand and began to push forward again.

"Sorry," she muttered, edging past a clutch of college students. "So sorry. I'm...trying to catch up to my husband."

She hoped God would forgive her the lie and that Tom wouldn't overhear her. "*Mi esposo está allá,*" she added and jerked her head toward the front of the line as she hurried on. "Excuse me. *Discúlpeme, por favor. Discúlpeme. Pardon. Mon mari. J'ai besoin de*...I need...*Necesito a...mi esposo...*" She babbled in Italian as well. It didn't matter now.

They were within a few yards of the doorway. She saw the border guards flicking cursory glances at the passports shoved at them, then waving people on.

"Please, let me by." Emily cast another desperate glance behind her. He was coming around the corner of the last lane of travelers. Frantic, she shoved onward, ignoring the mutters and grumbles. "I just have to reach my husband! Please. I don't know where he's got to. I—"

She smacked against a hard masculine chest, looked up past a firmly chiseled jaw and high cheekbones into startlingly blue, stony cold eyes. Her fingers curled against his shirtfront.

Did she dare?

She wasn't even sure she articulated the thought. It was instinct. Panic. And really, what choice did she have with Gomez on her heels?

"Thank God, darling," she babbled, throwing her arms around the stranger and hugging him hard. "I thought I'd lost you!"

CHAPTER TWO

EMILY tensed, expecting him to thrust her aside. The cold eyes flickered with surprise, then one dark brow arched and his mouth curved slightly at one corner.

"I hadn't known I was lost."

Thank heavens he spoke English. She'd have been in hot water over her eyeballs if he hadn't. But the words were reassuringly familiar even though the accent was definitely British.

Grateful not to have been rejected out of hand, Emily clung. "Er—well, you know how it is—how I am—about c-crowds and all. I didn't see you and——"

She had to stop babbling! The man would think she was a fool. She *was* a fool. But at least, she saw with a satisfied glance, Gomez appeared to be stopped in his tracks. He scowled at them.

Emily pressed closer, her lips against the stranger's shirt collar. "I'm sorry. I just need a bit of help. It won't take long."

She was startled to feel a hard arm come around her. "This sort of help I can manage," he said. And quite suddenly she felt his lips brush her cheek!

Emily jerked back, shivering at the unexpected touch of his mouth. Bob Duggan's kiss hadn't given her near the jolt this man's had.

"How's that?" he drawled. "That help?"

"Er..." Emily managed. She swallowed, flicked another glance at Gomez. The stranger's gaze followed hers, then looked back at her assessingly.

"I'm not sure he's convinced," he said, an unholy gleam in his eye. "That wasn't much of a kiss."

And before she could do a thing to stop him, he took another one!

Firm warm lips came down on hers, hard and insistent, demanding a response. And stunned, desperate, Emily gave him one.

Her eyes shut, and her lips parted, opening to him, just as if he were the man she'd been waiting for all her life.

She'd never kissed a man like that! Never even wanted to! Marc had always complained about her kisses. Icy Emily, he'd called her. He should see her now. She pushed back away from the stranger, frantic, amazed at the magnitude of her response.

"Relax." Strong fingers kneaded the taut cords of her neck. He nodded in the direction of the man who'd been pursuing her. "If you want to convince your friend, that is."

Emily had forgotten about Gomez!

Now, heart hammering, fighting against the persuasiveness of his touch, she shot a desperate glance over her shoulder and was relieved to see that Gomez, though still staring at them, looked doubtful now, a deepening frown creasing his face.

Tom was staring up at Emily, his mouth open, his eyes agog. His gaze swivelled to the stranger. "Who's he?"

"An...old friend," Emily said quickly. She shoved Tom ahead of her, gave her rescuer a brief grateful smile and edged forward, still shaken.

The stranger stayed right behind her. Emily could feel his hand against her back, steering her along just as if he really were her husband. She trembled slightly. Nerves, she told herself. Only nerves.

"Irate boyfriend?" the stranger murmured in her ear.

"Of course not."

"Don't tell me he caught you with his wife."

Emily gasped.

He gave her a sardonic grin and a negligent shrug. "You never know."

She glared at him. Those maddening fingers came up again to caress the back of her neck.

"Relax, sweetheart. I'll take care of you."

"I don't need you to take care of me," Emily said stiffly.

"No? Forgive me if I find that a little hard to believe."

"I just need to get across the border."

"Why?"

"It's a long story." And, thank heavens, before she had time to say more than that, they had passed by the guards and were out the other side, hurrying along the corridors, and heading toward the stairs to the platform where they would board the train to Geneva. She almost fainted with relief.

The stranger shored her up.

She pulled away. "Let me go. I'm fine."

"Of course you are." He held up her hand so they could both see it trembling. Emily grimaced.

"So, why don't you just tell me? What are you running away from?"

If he'd sounded the least bit sympathetic, Emily might have told him. If the truth were known, she would have liked nothing better than to throw herself on him and let him solve her problems. But he stood there so judgmentally, as if this were all her fault.

"It's not important."

"You were scared to death."

"I was not! I was just...just...trying to get away from a persistent jerk."

It wasn't precisely a lie. It was just a matter of interpretation. Gomez was a persistent jerk, and if he wasn't after her but after Tom, well, that wasn't the stranger's business.

While Tom went on ahead, she stopped at the foot of the stairs and turned back, lifting her gaze to meet the stranger's. His eyes were the most beautiful she'd ever seen. They were also the coldest. Even colder, she thought, than those of the nasty Señor Gomez. "Look," she said, "I've already said I'm sorry. I...I shouldn't have involved you. But it's over now. I appreciate your assistance, and now I'll be on my way. Thank you." She started past him, but he caught her arm.

"Hold on."

"What?" Emily demanded.

"You don't think you owe me?"

"I've said thank you."

"That's nice. It's not quite what I had in mind."

And before she could do more than blink, he had his arms around her and was kissing her again.

This kiss was hotter and hungrier than the last, as if her earlier response, eager though it had been, hadn't satisfied. His lips tasted, tormented. His tongue teased, cajoled. And Emily, desperate, fought him—and her own traitorous desires—every step of the way.

Finally she could do nothing else.

"Damn!" He pulled back, wiping a hand across his mouth. "You bit me, you little termagant."

"Damned right I did! Persistent jerks seem to abound hereabouts!" Emily countered roundly, infuriated. And turning on her heel, she stamped up the steps.

She didn't look back to see where he went. She didn't want to know. How on earth did she pick them? First Marc, then this...this insufferable creep. Just because she had needed a bit of help...!

She wiped a hand across her mouth, trying to rid herself of the taste, the memory of him.

Damn him!

She tried not to think about him. He didn't matter. What mattered was that she and Tom were free. Thanks to the obnoxious stranger, they had made it to France unimpeded. It would be a great deal harder for Alejandro Gomez to take Tom away from her outside of Spain.

At least now they had some breathing space. The overnight train to Geneva would give them even more.

"He must be a very good friend." Tom was looking up at her curiously.

Emily looked down, startled. "What?"

"You didn't seem to mind kissing him."

She felt hot blood in her cheeks. "I...told you, he's an old friend."

Tom shrugged. "Okay. I found our car." He pointed to the one just beyond the head of the stairs. "That's the right number, isn't it?"

Emily nodded. "You're really sharp."

Tom beamed, then surveyed the length of the train. "It's a long 'un. Can we walk to the end of it? Please? Can we?"

Emily wanted to say no. She wanted to tuck him safely away in their compartment and bolt the door until they were on their way. She wanted to sit down before she fell down. The stranger's kiss was still making her tremble. But Tom was so eager and he'd been so good.

"All right. But let's hurry. The train leaves in ten minutes and we still have to find our compartment."

"I can find it easy," Tom said confidently, setting off at a run toward the end of the train.

"Aren't you just a little tired?" Emily asked when, at the end, she finally caught up with him.

"Sorta. But we get to sleep on the train." Tom gave a happy skip. "That'll be super, won't it?"

"Yes." Emily needed a good night's sleep.

She made a lousy fugitive. She'd been running for scarcely more than three hours and already she felt as if she'd been on the road for years. She glanced at her watch. "We've got only a couple of minutes."

They were back with a minute to spare.

Tom took the reservation slip, flashed her a grin and pounded up the steep steps ahead of her. When she finally got up the steps and turned the corner, he was walking down the narrow corridor, standing on tiptoe outside every compartment, checking the numbers.

"*Aquí está*. Here it is!"

Emily compared the number on the reservation slip with the number on the compartment, then nodded. "You're right."

The train lurched and began to move.

Emily opened the door.

"You!"

There on the bottom bunk, his tie undone, his shirt unbuttoned, sat the infuriating stranger!

He gave her a typically infuriating grin and made a mocking little bow. "We have to stop meeting like this."

Furious, Emily averted her gaze, not wanting to see the wicked gleam in his eyes nor the visible expanse of hair-roughened chest. But dropping her gaze didn't help, for when she did she noticed that the top button on his pants was undone. "What are you...? You can't be here! You're in the wrong compartment!"

"No."

"This is our compartment!" She waved the reservation slip in his face.

He took it out of her hand, scanning it, then shrugging. "So it is." He smiled again. "Good thing we're married, isn't it?"

Emily started to splutter.

Tom giggled. "He's teasing you," he told Emily matter-of-factly, making her feel even more of a fool. He looked at the man. "Aren't you?" he asked.

The man regarded Tom solemnly for a moment, then reached out and tousled Tom's dark hair. "Of course."

He turned to Emily. "Even though I was here first, I'll be generous. You two can have whichever berths you want. I'll take what's left."

"You'll do no such thing! This is *our* compartment."

"And mine, too," he said simply and proffered a reservation slip of his own.

"There's been a mistake. There has to be! They wouldn't put you in with us! You'll have to find somewhere else."

"Have you ever tried finding a berth on a sleeper in the middle of summer without a reservation?"

"No, but——"

"Can't be done. Rarer than hen's teeth."

"Nonsense," Emily said briskly. "There's an extra one right here."

"Only because my... traveling companion couldn't make it."

It didn't take Emily much imagination to conjure up what sort of traveling companion hadn't been able to come along. She scowled.

The train was picking up speed even as they spoke.

"How unfortunate for you," she said icily.

"In the circumstances, it's probably just as well." He gave her a cool smile.

Emily bristled, catching his insinuation with no trouble at all. "Don't expect me to take her place!"

"Oh, I don't think you'd mind all that much."

"Go to hell," Emily muttered, and was even more furious with him when her words caused Tom to look at her, shocked.

"Sorry," she muttered. Here she was supposed to be feeling safe now that they were in France, and instead she felt as if her life was slipping totally out of control. "There must be a berth somewhere that you can use."

"You're welcome to try to find one."

"Fine." She took Tom by the hand. "Come on."

But Tom, for the first time that night, dug in his heels. "I want to stay here."

"Tom." Emily pulled him toward the door.

"Let him stay," the man suggested. "He's probably exhausted, poor kid."

"He's——"

"I'm tired," Tom said as if on cue.

"You're fine. I don't——"

"What's the matter?" the man challenged. "Do you think I'll steal him?"

"I don't think *you'll* steal him," Emily said sharply, and regretted her emphasis the moment the words were out of her mouth.

Tom looked instantly worried. Emily shut her eyes and tried to regain control. "Nobody's going to steal you," she said to Tom, then raked a hand through her hair. "Nobody's going to steal him," she repeated firmly for the benefit of the interloper. "But he's coming with me."

"But——" Tom protested.

"Now."

He continued to look mulish, but Emily wasn't budging. She jerked open the door.

"Never mind. I'll look," the stranger said gruffly. "You wait here."

"Thank you."

He gave her a grim smile. "Do you mind if I leave my bags here while I'm gone?"

She shook her head. "Please do."

"Thank you very much." There was irony in his tone, too, but she was too tired to care.

"I thought you said he was your friend?" Tom pointed out as soon as the man had left. "You kissed him."

"Yes, well, that doesn't mean we're going to sleep with him. He shouldn't be sharing our compartment."

"But it's his, too," Tom protested.

"Not for long, I hope. Come on. Let's get you into your pyjamas and you can go to bed."

Tom, having admitted to being tired and fascinated with the idea of actually sleeping on the train, didn't argue. He changed quickly. Then, while he went to brush his teeth, Emily took advantage of his absence to get ready for bed herself.

Wearily she stripped off her dress and bra, opened her duffel, then pulled out the elongated T-shirt she intended to sleep in.

It was over her head when the door opened. "Back already?" she asked through the folds of cotton. "That was fast."

"I'd have been quicker if I'd known what was waiting." The voice was an octave deeper than Tom's.

Emily yanked the T-shirt all the way on and glared into the stranger's eyes. Her face flamed. "You could have knocked."

"And miss the floor show? No way. Besides, I should think you'd be used to it. I'm surprised you care."

"Why shouldn't I care? A man I don't even know walks in when I'm barely dressed, and I'm not supposed to care?"

"You don't care when you model, do you?"

She stiffened. "How do you know I model?"

"I've seen your...face." The way his eyes traveled the length of her body and the discreet pause in his words let her know that wasn't all he'd seen. Damn him. Was she really that recognizable? That memorable?

"That's different," she said shortly. "Besides, I don't model any more."

He cocked his head. "No? Why not?"

She folded her clothes and put them into her bag, keeping her back to him. "I have other priorities. Not that it's any of your business."

"Tom?"

She spun around. "How did you know his name?"

"You called him by it." His tone was patient. The look in his eyes was not.

She felt suddenly foolish. "Oh, yes. Of course."

"But surely you had him while you were still modeling?"

"He's...not my son. He's my nephew. I'm his guardian." She didn't want to explain any more. She reached for his suitcases. "Here. You'll be wanting these."

He took them and stowed them underneath the berth.

"What are you doing?" Emily demanded.

"Couldn't find room at the inn. I told you I wouldn't be able to."

"I'll bet you didn't even look."

He opened the door. "Look yourself, then, sweetheart."

She was about to. But just then Tom came back, and behind him she saw Gomez—coming down the corridor. The color drained from her face.

She yanked Tom in and shut the door at once, twisting the lock and putting her back against it.

"Another persistent jerk?" The stranger mocked her.

Emily glared.

Tom looked up at him quizzically. "Are you staying?"

The man looked at Emily, a sardonic smile twisting his mouth. He waited.

Emily met his gaze, then let hers slide away. She drew a breath. "He's staying," she said.

"Imagine that," the man murmured.

Gritting her teeth, Emily ignored him. She bustled about in the cramped space, boosting Tom up to tuck him into the upper berth he had chosen. Then, turning her back to their new compartment mate, she slipped quickly into her own below.

For a long moment he just stood there. Resolutely Emily faced the wall, holding her breath. If he reached for her, touched her, she'd scream.

He reached over and flicked out the light.

Emily lay in the darkness that was supposed to be her refuge and knew for a fact that it was not.

There was nothing remotely comforting about hearing the clink of his belt buckle, the rasp of his zip, the soft sounds of him fumbling with his buttons, unlacing his shoes.

"You don't have to get undressed," she hissed at him.

"You want to do it for me?"

She gave an irritated wuffle. He laughed.

He was so close she could feel the heat from his body as he moved in the tiny space. Her fingers tightened on the sheet. Then his pants hit the floor, the berth right opposite creaked and he slipped beneath the blanket.

"You know," he said conversationally, "I've never slept with someone to whom I've never been properly introduced."

"You're not sleeping with me!"

"Close. But not close enough."

"Far too close," Emily gritted.

"Do you think so?" His voice was softly mocking. "We'll see." He was silent for a moment, then said, "So, what's your name, pretty lady?"

She debated lying to him, then decided not to bother. "Emily Musgrave, not that it makes a bit of difference."

"Oh, it does," he said. "A world of difference. Pleased to meet you, Emily Musgrave." He paused, then added, "After all this time."

Emily frowned. "All what time?"

"Why, all the time I've seen you staring at me from magazines and such."

"That's not me," she muttered.

"Really?" He didn't sound as if he believed her. He rolled over onto his side so that he faced her. She refused to look at him, stared instead up at the dark form of the berth above her head.

"Who are you, then?" he asked her.

"Never mind. It's not important."

"I think it is," he said. His voice was silky. "And if you won't tell me, I guess I'll just have to find out."

She heard both seduction and threat in his words. Or thought she did. Heavens, she was confused tonight.

"Who are you?" she asked grudgingly after a moment. She didn't really want to know, didn't want to pursue the acquaintance any further than it had already gone, which was much too far. But she needed a name, some way to pigeonhole him, control the effect he had on her.

"MacPherson," he said. "Sandy MacPherson. You can call me Mac," he added softly. "All my wives do."

It was not the getaway Emily had planned.

MacPherson rolled over in his berth and, seconds later, was snoring, while for hours Emily lay stiff and unmoving in hers, feeling with her whole body the whoosh and thrum of the train as it sped through tunnel and countryside, aware with her whole mind of the man lying just inches away from her.

Sandy MacPherson. Mac.

No, her mind instantly corrected. *Mr.* MacPherson.

Even if "all his wives" did call him Mac, she certainly wasn't going to!

Was he married?

Somehow she doubted it. Though he was certainly sexy and attractive enough to have had his fair share of women dangling after him, there was nothing domesticated about Sandy MacPherson.

Sandy didn't fit him. It made him sound gentle, domestic, like a tabby cat perhaps. But there was nothing tabbylike about him. He was far more the dangerous jungle cat, hungry and on the prowl. She didn't think there was much chance that he went docilely home to one particular hearthside every night.

She had really done it when she'd latched on to him. It had been sheer stupidity to do so. Look where it had got her! Out of the frying pan into the fire.

She had enough on her plate right now, trying to take care of Tom and avoid Gomez, without having a man like MacPherson around to complicate things.

And she had no doubt that he intended to complicate them. That mocking grin and those hard blue eyes told her quite clearly that he thought she was ripe for the picking. She knew that her modeling career made her seem fair game to lots of men. She must be fast and loose if she let her body be photographed and displayed for the world—that was what most people seemed to think.

Certainly that was what Marc had thought.

He'd been amazed at first by her scrupulously proper behavior. But it hadn't put him off, so she'd thought he must be pleased. She hadn't realized he was busy getting his loving elsewhere.

She didn't make the mistake of thinking that MacPherson was pleased by her behavior. It must annoy him a great deal, especially when she'd flung her arms around him in the first place. Some men might have called it provocative, might have accused her of leading them on. Men expected sex as payment for everything, she thought irritably.

"Tough," she muttered, even though she felt faintly guilty for her actions. She owed him a thank-you, nothing more.

She punched her pillow and tried to go to sleep. She didn't have a prayer.

It was because of Gomez, she told herself. It was because she wasn't cut out to be a fugitive, because she was worried about Tom, because she was scared.

But it wasn't Gomez she was thinking about. Or Tom.

And if she was scared it had nothing to do with either of them. It had entirely to do with the man in the bunk next to hers—and with the way she'd reacted to him.

Carefully, quietly, she rolled onto her back, then turned her head just enough so that she could glimpse his profile in the darkness. He had shifted over onto his side, so all she could really see was a large lump just opposite. It didn't matter. She didn't need light to remember the way he looked—nor the way he'd looked at her when he'd come in and found her half dressed. There had been hunger in his gaze. And disdain. There had been curiosity. And desire. His eyes had made her shiver with their intensity and their coldness. And yet, once or twice, for a fleeting instant, she'd thought she'd glimpsed a flame.

She remembered the way they had skated over her, tracing the tilt of her chin, the lift of her breasts, the curve of her hips.

The world had seen more of her in swimsuit ads than MacPherson had. Yet never had she felt so exposed.

Damn the man.

Damn all men, for that matter, Emily thought irritably. Sandy MacPherson, Bob Duggan and, most especially, that miserable rotten Alejandro Gomez, who was making all this necessary.

Sleep, she counseled herself. Sleep and forget them.

She sighed, rolled over and punched her pillow. The train whooshed into another tunnel, rattling the windows and making her ears pop. Tom whimpered softly in his sleep. MacPherson snored.

It was going to be a very long night.

It wasn't yet light when the train stopped in Lyons, but Emily was awake. Again. Or, perhaps, still.

Whoever said that the soft sway and lulling clickety-clack of nighttime train travel were instant sleep inducers obviously hadn't experienced what she had. Or maybe his compartment had been air-conditioned and his sleeping companions less noisy. Or maybe he hadn't been worried that the shadow passing the door every so often was Alejandro Gomez.

Probably, she thought in retrospect, it had been a mistake to open the door and peek out the first time she'd seen the shadow. If she hadn't, she never would have seen his back disappearing into the compartment four doors down. She might not have sat huddled and fretting for the better part of the night, until MacPherson's gruff, "For heaven's sake, go to sleep," sent her skittering under the blanket.

He'd rolled over and glared at her. "Stop worrying. I'll protect you, pretty lady."

But Emily didn't think she believed that. Oh, he might protect her from Gomez, all right. But who was going to protect her from him?

Now she stared out at Lyons's mostly deserted Part-Dieu station and wondered if she ought to wake Tom and get off. If she did, would she be home free?

Possibly. At least as far as MacPherson went. But there were drawbacks, too.

She didn't know a soul in Lyons. She'd have to check into a hotel, and there she'd be far easier to find than if she were able to stay with friends. If she could get to Guido's, it would be much better. But could she get to Guido's?

She probably could if she stayed with MacPherson. Gomez hadn't seized her in Cerbère, she suspected, because she'd clung so tightly to MacPherson and if he'd tried to interfere there would have been a scene.

Gomezes, she gathered, didn't like scenes. They were the bastions of propriety, according to her sister-in-law. Proper, dignified, never willing to air their grievances in public. They just made you miserable in private, she thought grimly.

"Now what?"

Emily started, then turned to find MacPherson raised up on one elbow, scowling at her.

It was still scarcely light and she couldn't make out his features well, only the rumpled state of his dark hair and the shadowy darkness along his jaw. He looked more predatory than ever. She tucked the blanket more closely around her. "Nothing. I don't sleep well on trains."

"Nor do I."

"That wasn't you I heard snoring?" she said tartly.

A grin flashed in the darkness. "I was faking." He sat up and the blanket fell away. She saw that he was bare-chested, experienced the same sudden shortness of breath she'd felt last night, and hastily averted her eyes. She expected him to remark on her prudishness and was relieved when he didn't.

"You're getting off in Geneva?"

"I might get off here."

"That's a stupid idea."

She bristled. "What do you know about it?"

"I know you're running."

"I'm not——"

"And if you're running, you need a plan," he went on, just as if she hadn't spoken. "You can't just dash around willy-nilly dragging the boy with you." He sounded calm, matter-of-fact, as if runaway females were not all that unusual in his life.

Perhaps, Emily thought grimly, they weren't.

"So what do you suggest?" she asked gruffly.

"That you stop springing up like a jack-in-the-box every time you see that dark-haired fellow. It's making me dizzy and it's not doing you a damned bit of good. If you need to get away from him, you have to stop calling attention to yourself."

"You know a lot about that, do you?" Emily asked sourly.

"A fair bit."

"You plan lots of escapes?"

He smiled. "Some."

"Member of British Intelligence, I suppose?" she sniffed.

He shook his head. "A writer."

She stared. He looked as much like her idea of a writer as she resembled a frumpy *hausfrau*. Writers wore tweedy jackets with leather elbow patches. They smoked pipes and had bald patches.

"What do you write? Men's erotic fantasies? Chance encounters in the railway station?"

"There's an idea!" He leered. "Want to try a little research?"

Emily, wishing she'd kept her mouth shut, held the blanket close against her breasts. "Very funny."

"I doubt it would be funny at all." His tone shifted and there was a soft seductiveness in it now that made Emily both aware and anxious at the same time. "I think it would be marvelous."

"Stop it," she muttered.

His grin vanished and he gave her a long, assessing look. "You're an odd duck, you know that," he said almost conversationally. "Most models don't blush and go all frantic when a man looks at them."

Emily scowled. "You know all about models, too, do you?"

"I've dated a few."

She didn't doubt it. Most of the ones she knew would have jumped at a chance to date a man as good-looking as this one. "For research purposes?" she asked tartly.

"No." He grinned wickedly. "But I've probably used a bit of the material unintentionally."

"And you'll use this, too, I suppose."

"Nothing's happened. Yet."

"Nothing's going to happen!"

"Then you don't have anything to worry about, do you?"

The train began to move again. Emily sighed and looked away at the station as they picked up speed and moved away. "Much you know," she muttered.

MacPherson leaned forward, wrapping his arms around his knees. Emily could feel his gaze on her and she deliberately looked away.

"What's this guy got on you, Emily Musgrave?"

She didn't answer.

"It's more than just unrequited love, isn't it?"

She hunched her shoulders. "Why? Do you want to use it in a book?"

"I never use real people. The places are real. The details are. The stories are pure imagination."

"Then why?"

He shrugged. "I thought maybe I could help you plan."

She examined his words for undercurrents and was surprised not to find any. He hadn't been exactly a knight in shining armor so far. Still, he didn't seem wholly willing to pitch her into the arms of her adversary. Maybe if she could...

"No." It was too tempting. It would be too easy. Tom was her responsibility, no one else's. Besides, her reactions to MacPherson were far too volatile. "You've helped enough, thanks." She turned her head and stared out of the window again, afraid of saying more.

They were heading out of the city now, big buildings and apartment houses giving way to small family dwellings.

"I have," he agreed after a moment. "So you owe me."

Emily's gaze snapped back to meet his. "Not another kiss!"

He grinned. "I thought it wasn't bad at all, myself, but if you'd rather, I'll settle for something else this time."

"What?"

"An explanation."

She knew he wouldn't leave off, retire gracefully, admit defeat. His kind never did. She sighed. "I... have something he wants."

"Tom."

She gave a little jerk. "How do you know?"

"What else? You aren't wearing the Crown Jewels, and you're far too skittish to be running drugs. You'd be picked up in a minute. So, who is he?"

Emily looked out of the window. "My sister-in-law's brother. I think."

"You don't know?" He sounded incredulous.

"I've never met him," Emily admitted. "I suppose it could be one of his henchmen," she added defensively. "But something tells me it's Gomez in the flesh. Goose bumps or something. I think I get them whenever he's close." Emily tried to smile, but it wasn't funny. Nothing about Alejandro Gomez was funny.

"And he wants Tom?"

"Yes."

MacPherson shifted and leaned against the wall of the compartment. "If you're his guardian, what's the problem?"

"It won't stop him."

MacPherson lifted a sardonic brow. "Who is he? A Mafia don?"

"Might as well be. His name is Alejandro Gomez. He and his family practically own half the business interests in Madrid. They have company branches in every major city in Spain. They have corporate offices in London and Paris, Rio and Singapore. I think they own the world."

MacPherson laughed. "I think you exaggerate."

"Maybe. But suffice it to say they have a damned sight more influence than I do. Particularly in Spain."

"But if your guardianship is legal...? Or have you perhaps given him reason to contest it? Maybe you've led a less than pure life, Emily Musgrave?" The insinuation in his voice infuriated her.

"I have not!" Emily could scarcely keep her voice down.

"Right," he drawled. "You do resemble purity personified."

"Think whatever you like," she said stiffly, "it won't change what I am."

"I never imagined it would," he said easily. "So if you're pure and blameless, what chance has he got?"

"Less now that I'm in France," she admitted. "But he's still here. I thought he'd leave. The fact that he hasn't worries me. He might try something. Might...try to take Tom away physically."

"You're sure he wants to take him away from you?"

"What else would he want?"

MacPherson shrugged. "Visiting rights?"

Emily snorted. "He never wanted them before. It isn't as if he cared about Tom before Mari died. That's my sister-in-law," she explained, and he nodded curtly.

"When did she die?"

"About five months ago."

"Of what?"

"She had a rare blood disease. When she knew there was no hope for recovery, she asked me to come and take care of her and Tom."

"And you just dropped everything and came?" She could hear the skepticism in his voice.

"Yes. It—it was a good time for me to get away," she added honestly.

A corner of his mouth lifted in a smile that wasn't precisely pleasant. "Right. You were jilting somebody about that time, weren't you?"

She stared. "How did you——?"

"I read the papers. Like everyone else."

"I broke off my engagement."

"Left him at the altar."

"You don't know everything."

"Enough. You are a relatively famous lady. Or should I say, infamous?"

"Don't say anything!" She scowled at him, then drew her knees up to her chest and hugged them tightly. Roll on Geneva, she thought.

"So go on," MacPherson said after a moment. "You selflessly went to nurse your sister-in-law——"

"I did the best I could," she said sharply. "I loved her. I love Tom. That's why she left him to me. She wanted Tom to be raised by the person who loved him most!"

"What happened to Tom's father?"

"David was a navy pilot. He died three years ago in a crash."

MacPherson frowned. She couldn't tell what he was thinking. He had one of those enigmatic faces, determinedly indecipherable. "It must have been rough for the boy," he said after a moment. "That's a lot to lose in such a short life."

"Yes. That's another reason I'm not letting anyone take him from me. He's just getting adjusted again after his mother's death. Can you imagine what it would be like for him to be yanked away from me and given to people he's never seen before?"

"Why hasn't he?"

"Because as far as the Gomezes were concerned, he didn't exist."

She saw MacPherson's jaw tighten and went on to explain, "They didn't approve of David and Marielena getting married, didn't think he was good enough for her. The Gomezes are very conscious of their lineage. An American simply wasn't good enough for them! They're not pure Spanish themselves. But the part that isn't, according to Marielena, is some sort of English or French nobility." Emily's mouth twisted bitterly. "If you can't marry a duke, don't marry at all, seems to be that family motto."

"Interesting philosophy."

Emily snorted. "Stupid, if you ask me. They never even wanted to meet David. Just told Marielena that if she married him she might as well be dead as far as they were concerned. And they meant it. She never heard from them again." Her fingers clenched on the blanket and she stared unseeing out of the window.

The countryside was bathed now in the soft glow of early morning light. Snowcapped peaks loomed in the distance.

"But when she really did die, suddenly everything changed," she went on hoarsely. "They found out about Tom and wanted him. They tried to take over. Wanted his school bills sent to them. Wanted his reports. Sent people to the school to try to talk to him. Came by our apartment."

"Then why haven't you met him?"

"I told you! I wasn't letting him near Tom. I don't trust him. In Spain, what Alejandro Gomez wants, Alejandro Gomez gets."

"But not in Geneva?"

Emily's chin jutted. Her fists clenched. She met MacPherson's gaze firmly and squarely. "Not in Geneva. Or anywhere else."

CHAPTER THREE

IF ONLY it were that simple.

But an hour later, when Emily gathered up Tom and the bags and bade a brief, somewhat stiff farewell to Sandy MacPherson at the door of the train and hurried along the platform toward Customs, she knew it would not be.

There, just beyond the Customs men, already leaning against a wall and scanning the crowds that passed, exactly as she had feared, stood Alejandro Gomez.

Emily pulled up short, looking desperately for another way out.

There wasn't one.

Oh, help, Emily thought and, just as she did so, heard behind her an all too familiar voice. "Lost me again, did you?"

Tom turned. "Hi, Mac! Are you coming with us?"

MacPherson looked at Emily. Slowly his gaze traveled past her toward the man leaning against the wall, then just as slowly it moved lazily back to focus on her again. "I don't know. Am I?"

Emily's own gaze went to the heavens. But all the divine intervention it appeared she was going to get was standing right smack in front of her, his blue eyes challenging her.

She had no desire to tangle with him. All she could hope was that Gomez had none either. She drew a deep breath, then gave him her sunniest smile. "I believe you are."

His own smile was knowing as he reached for her bag and took her arm with his.

She saw Gomez frown and start forward. MacPherson's jaw tightened and the hard blue eyes focused right on Gomez for an instant, seeming almost to dare him to interfere.

To Emily's giddy relief, the other man looked away first. She breathed a sigh of relief.

They got through Customs without a hitch, MacPherson playing his part to the hilt. His hand slipped away from her arm to rest against the small of her back, his face was so close to hers that his breath fanned her ear.

Emily's pulses raced. From the close encounter with Gomez, she assured herself. Certainly not from MacPherson's close proximity.

But she was glad when they finally rounded the corner, merged into the morning rush-hour crowd of pedestrians, and the dark-haired man disappeared from view so that she could pull away and breathe more easily.

"Where to?" MacPherson asked her.

"Taxi. But you needn't come with us." She might as well have saved her breath.

"Where are you going?"

"A friend of mine—a photographer—lives here."

"Evans?"

Emily looked at him, surprised at the harshness of his tone. "Howell? Do you know him?"

"Of him." Whatever he knew, it didn't sound as if he liked it.

"Howell lives in Wales," Emily said. "This is Guido Farantino. Do you know him?"

"No." He was scowling now as they shoved through the crowd. Emily could still feel his hand, hard and warm, against her back.

It was disconcerting how strongly she reacted to his touch. When Bob Duggan touched her, she felt nothing. When most men touched her she felt nothing. The last person who had made her tingle with awareness had been Marc.

And she would do well to remember that, she thought grimly.

At least when they got to the taxi lineup, he'd go his own way. "Wonderful," she said when they arrived. "We've made it. Thank you very much."

"You're quite welcome," MacPherson said, but his hand stayed right where it was.

"You needn't hang around, Mr. MacPherson."

He was still scowling. "I told you, my name is Mac. And I'm not 'hanging around,' sweetheart. I'm waiting for a taxi."

She felt hot blood rise in her cheeks. "Of course." Her fingers twisted on the strap of her bag. Idiot, she chastised herself.

Fortunately the line moved quickly and before long the next taxi was theirs. Or would have been if MacPherson hadn't climbed in after them!

Emily stopped. "What the——?"

He shoved her in. "Get going."

"But——"

"You have company," MacPherson said, jerking his head toward the back of the queue. "Or maybe you don't care."

Emily glanced toward the rear of the line, knowing whom she would see, and not surprised to find him there. Her mustachioed nemesis was staring right at her. She started to tremble.

"Who's following us?" Tom wanted to know, scrambling up onto his knees and peering around curiously.

"Never mind, Tom," Emily said. The last thing she wanted was him worrying.

But Tom was not deterred. "That guy?" The boy pointed at Gomez. "I've seen him before."

Emily sighed. "At Cerbère last night."

"Before that. At school."

Emily's teeth clenched. So she'd been right. Gomez had been trying to infiltrate Tom's life for weeks now.

MacPherson's fingers came up to massage the taut cords of her neck. "Probably just someone who looks like him," he said to Tom, and to Emily, "Calm down. Think about something else."

Emily glared at him. "What?"

"This." And before she could move, his lips touched hers. It was a very persuasive kiss. It spoke of hunger and desire and need. It reminded her of all the feelings he'd excited in her last night, feelings she'd been trying to assure herself were nothing more than the product of tension and stress and an overstimulated imagination.

It gave Emily far more to think about than she'd ever wanted! Her mind reeled.

The driver slipped into the front seat. "*Où allez-vous?*"

MacPherson lifted his head and looked at her expectantly.

Emily stared back, unseeing. She knew what he was asking, she just couldn't form the words.

"The address?" Mac coaxed.

Face flaming, she dug through her purse and found Guido's address, then handed it to the driver, who looked at it, nodded and pulled away from the curb.

"That's better," MacPherson breathed into her ear.

Emily wasn't sure about that.

The streets, clogged with morning traffic and road-repair crews, made their progress slow. But gradually they skirted Lake Geneva, heading out into the residential area.

Emily didn't know how far it was to Guido's house, but they couldn't get there quickly enough as far as she was concerned. It wasn't only going to be her haven in which to hide from Gomez. She needed to get away from MacPherson!

He was the wrong man in the wrong place at the wrong time.

There was nothing right about him at all.

Except the way he kissed.

It would be a good thing when she got to Guido's and could say goodbye to Mr. Sandy MacPherson. He was far too attractive, far too charming, far too sexy for Emily's own good.

She didn't like men like him, men who could make the world jump to their wishes, men whose strength and charisma was all too obvious. Men like Marc and Alejandro Gomez, who used people for their own ends and didn't really care about them as human beings.

You thought his strength was nice when you needed it, she reminded herself, to be fair. And of course that was true. But that didn't mean she wanted to continue the acquaintance.

She slanted him a glance. He was looking at Tom, and she saw a faint softening in his features as he did so, a hint of gentleness that seemed entirely out of character.

He looked like a pirate. Or a highwayman. She had a hard time imagining him as a dreamy, nonactive writer.

"What sort of books do you write?" she asked him. She might, she thought, find one some day. Read it. Remember.

"Don't say you believe me after all."

She flushed and shrugged, remembering her skepticism last night. What if he really did write erotic stories?

"I write spy thrillers, Emily Musgrave."

"I read spy thrillers," Emily told him. "I don't remember any by Sandy MacPherson or Sanford MacPherson or whatever your name is."

"Dominic Piersall."

She goggled. "Dominic Piersall? *You're* Dominic Piersall?"

For the first time since she'd met him, he looked slightly embarrassed. "On paper, I am."

"Heavens."

Dominic Piersall was just about the best known of the new breed of thriller writers to have come out of Britain in the post Cold-War period. Unlike the purveyors of the techno-thriller, he concentrated heavily on men and their motivations. And he did it better than anyone going as far as Emily and many other readers were concerned.

Dominic Piersall had devious clever plots that grew out of the machinations of devious, clever, all too believable characters. The biggest criticism leveled at him was that he wrote so slowly. A new book every couple of years was about all his most devoted fans could expect. Emily looked at him with awe.

Kissed by Dominic Piersall? She couldn't stifle the giggle.

"You think it's funny?"

She shook her head quickly. "Not a bit. You're famous."

"It's no big deal."

"Maybe you don't think so, but..." She felt suddenly awkward, aware of him in yet another way. "I didn't know. I'm sorry to have bothered you like this. I never would have, if I'd known."

"Why? I'm not a mortal man any more? I could have declined."

"Yes, but——"

His blue eyes nailed her. "If you hadn't, Emily Musgrave, I'd have simply had to contrive some other way to meet you."

The implication was too blatant to miss. It was nothing she hadn't heard from countless other men, Marc included. So why, this time, did it send a funny little quiver down her spine before she deliberately made herself stiffen and swallow hard?

"*Vous êtes là.*"

Thank God. She didn't say it, but she certainly thought it, as she gave herself a little jerk, then tore her gaze away from MacPherson's.

Startled back to the moment, Emily looked around. The taxi had stopped outside a four-story cream stucco apartment house and the driver was looking back at her expectantly. "*Vous êtes là*," he repeated.

"Oh—er—*oui. Merci.*"

"Is this it?" Tom looked around curiously.

But before Emily could reply, MacPherson said, "No."

She blinked. "But——"

He jerked his head in the direction of the cross street. "Look. Up near the corner."

Emily followed his gaze. She saw another taxi parked by a streetlight. And in the back there sat watching them, a familiar-looking dark-haired man.

No, she thought. It couldn't be! How had he known?

She wanted to scream. To cry.

Before she could do more than draw a breath, Mac spoke rapidly to the driver in French. The driver shrugged, then grunted a response, backed the car up and shot around the corner, heading back from where they'd come.

Emily was shaking. How had he known about Guido?

She'd told no one. Had he tailed them? But he seemed to have arrived before they did. Did he have spies in her brain? Did he know every person she had ever met?

Emily felt an impotent fury rising inside her, coupled with a sensation of growing helplessness.

"What am I going to do?" And though she hated the thread of panic in her voice, she couldn't squelch it.

"Simple," MacPherson said as he settled back in the seat beside her. "You're coming with me."

They couldn't afford a room at the small exclusive lakefront hotel where Mac had reserved a room. "We'll go some place cheaper," Emily said when the taxi pulled up out front.

But MacPherson contradicted her. "Don't be stupid. How am I supposed to keep an eye on you if you're staying halfway across town?"

"You don't need to keep an eye on us."

"I'm glad to hear it," he said dryly, steering her up a flight of wide stone steps even as she protested. "Now come along, and stop worrying. I have a suite."

"I do not intend to impose on you," she said as he led her through the dark wooden door.

"You're not imposing. You're invited."

"No."

Mac stopped suddenly in the middle of the Aubusson-carpeted foyer and turned to face her. "Got a better idea?"

The direct challenge removed what little wind was left in Emily's sails.

She had no other ideas.

She hadn't thought beyond getting to Guido's. From there, she had been certain, she could have come up with a game plan, contacted her lawyer in the States, received some advice as to how to thwart her powerful adversary.

Now she couldn't even get there without running the gauntlet set up by Alejandro Gomez.

She blinked tiredly, the days of worry and the night without sleep catching up with her all at once. MacPherson staring down at her, powerful and challenging, didn't help in the least. She simply sagged where she stood.

"Right," MacPherson said.

And before she knew what was happening, he steered both her and Tom up a short flight of stairs to a heavy walnut door which he opened.

"In," he commanded, and Emily found herself in a small, tastefully furnished sitting room with tall narrow windows overlooking the lake.

The entire suite spoke not of glitz, but of elegance and quiet good taste. It was warm and welcoming, like a safe harbor in a storm-swept sea. MacPherson pointed her toward a tapestry-covered wing chair. "Sit."

"I'm not a dog," she complained as she sat.

"No. Dogs mind better."

Tom giggled, and Emily shot him a dark look.

Mac tousled the little boy's hair. "Are you hungry?"

Tom nodded emphatically.

Mac crossed the room and picked up the phone, then spoke rapidly in French. "Breakfast in twenty minutes, old man," he promised when he hung up. "In the meantime, how about a bath?"

To Emily's everlasting astonishment, Tom agreed.

While she sat in a tired stupor, he went off happily with Mac, chattering at length about the fleet of boats for the tub he had at home in Barcelona.

"This is a huge tub," she heard Tom say to him. "Do you have a bathtub this big?"

"Pretty close."

"Where do you live?"

"In England most of the time. Sometimes in Spain. Now and then in Singapore. I get around."

Emily supposed he must. His books went all over the world. The last one she'd read, a spine-tingler called *Dominos*, had moved around the Far East with the ease of someone familiar with the area. His first book, she recalled, had been set in Spain.

"In houses? Or apartments?" Tom didn't care at all about MacPherson's globe-trotting activities. He loved the idea of a house with a huge garden. He'd never had one, and, to his child's mind, heaven would be a place with huge trees to climb, a room of his own with a window overlooking a lake, and a pony to ride every day after school.

Emily knew they'd never have all that. But the house was within the realm of possibility, even though it was a long way off.

"I have a little apartment in Singapore. The others are houses," MacPherson said.

"Big 'uns?"

"Monstrous old things, both of 'em."

"Really?" Tom sounded awed. "Which is your favorite?"

"The one in England. It belonged to my mother's family. Six bedrooms. A big kitchen. Nice grounds. A horse paddock and plenty of room to ride. You like to ride?"

"I... never have," Tom confided wistfully.

"We'll have to change that."

Emily stiffened. How dared he get Tom's hopes up like that? She wanted to speak up, but she didn't want him to know she'd been eavesdropping.

She also didn't want to stop.

She wanted to know all she could about MacPherson.

She knew precious little so far. He was a hard man, she could tell that simply by looking at him. She didn't think he suffered fools gladly, and she wasn't quite sure why he was bothering with her. Sometimes she didn't even think he liked her. And then he kissed her!

But a man didn't have to like you to kiss you, as Emily well knew.

Maybe it had nothing to do with her. Maybe he felt sorry for Tom. It was easy enough to do—Tom was a likable child.

She was somewhat surprised that MacPherson had gained Tom's confidence so easily. Her nephew had not, since his mother's death, been very outgoing or willing to meet new people. Emily had put it down to a fear that any new friends might be lost to him the way his mother had. She hoped he wouldn't be hurt when they went their way and MacPherson went his. It would help if MacPherson would stop promising him treats.

She was still fuming about that when he came back into the room a few minutes later.

"Don't look so happy," he chided.

Emily made a face at him. "I'm not."

"Why not? You've eluded your pursuer so far. You've landed in a perfectly decent hotel suite. You're about to be fed a full English breakfast."

"And I'm becoming more and more beholden to a tyrannical man."

"Are you?" He rubbed his hands together. "Oh, good."

"You're enjoying this, aren't you?" she accused him. "It probably goes with being a spy novelist. Rescuing damsels in distress. Plotting and conniving escapes."

He sank down into a chair and stretched his long legs out in front of him. "I do admit to some expertise."

"I suppose you've rescued lots of women?"

"One or two." He gave her a wicked grin. "But you're the prettiest."

Emily looked away, hating the blush she knew suffused her cheeks.

"That was a compliment," MacPherson said. "You're supposed to say 'thank you,' Emily Musgrave. You have to learn to be gracious."

"I am gracious," she retorted, shooting him a glare.

One skeptical brow lifted, and she remembered all the ungracious things she'd said to him over the last half a day. "Sometimes," she qualified.

"We'll work on it. But first we need to make some plans."

"*We* don't need anything," Emily said sharply. "This is my problem."

"Gracious, gracious," he chided.

Emily scowled at him. She bit her thumbnail.

"It was your problem. You involved me. Now it's mine." His tone didn't brook any argument.

Emily argued anyway. "I never meant——"

"That wasn't you clutching my shirt, telling me you'd lost me?"

"Once! Once, for a matter of moments I involved you. That doesn't mean——"

"And this morning? Going from the train to the taxi? How about after we got to your friend's house?"

"A gentleman wouldn't harp on these things."

"Ah, but I never claimed to be a gentleman."

"Bully for you," Emily muttered with stubborn bad grace. She knew she should be grateful for his help. Dammit, she *was* grateful. She just didn't want to be beholden. Especially to him. It was too dangerous, attracted as she was to him.

"Now, if you're done fussing, we need to plan," he said mildly after a moment.

Emily pressed her lips together. "Fine. Plan away. I'm not exactly conversant with these sorts of intrigues. I've never had occasion to be before this."

"That's why you need me. Pay attention to a master."

She made a face at him.

"Do you want to stay one jump ahead of your Señor Gomez or not?"

"Of course I do."

"Then listen up. Today we can stay here, lie low, give Tom a chance to stretch his legs, give you a chance to take a nap. Don't deny you could use one," he said when she opened her mouth to protest. "And tomorrow we can take a bus to Chamonix."

"Chamonix? Why Chamonix?" Emily had heard of the well-known ski and alpine mountaineering town high in the Savoyard Alps. But she'd never been there and she certainly didn't know why she should go now.

"Because it's out of the way. It's a good place to take a break, relax a little, have some fun. And because I have a place there."

"You have places everywhere—Spain, England, Singapore..." she said without thinking.

"Doing a little eavesdropping, were you?"

She stiffened. "Just sitting here minding my own business. You were talking loud."

"Of course." His knowing smile annoyed her. "I also rent an apartment in Chamonix. I ski there in winter. I use it in the summer to write."

"Well, then, of course *you* should go there."

"We're all going."

"It's not necessary. You aren't obliged to us in the least. Really. We've imposed far too much and——"

"Shut up, Emily," he suggested conversationally.

She gaped at him, then did no such thing. "We don't need your help," she insisted. "Not any more, I mean," she added hastily, because of course they already had more times than she wanted to admit.

"But I need you."

Emily stared. Her protests stopped, her mouth hung open. "I beg your pardon."

She expected him to say he'd misspoken, but he only nodded gravely and repeated, "I need you."

"For what? Research?" she asked after a moment, her question mingled with a giddy half laugh.

Mac shrugged. "If you like." He paused, his gaze catching hers, holding it. "But there's more than that, too. And you know it."

Time seemed suddenly to stop.

No, Emily thought. Oh, no.

But she couldn't deny it. She did know, and, if she hadn't, the look he gave her was enough to tell her exactly what he meant. It was stark and hungry and spoke of things she'd only once dared dream of. And what a disaster that had been. She looked away.

"Emily."

She shook her head.

"You can't deny it."

"Don't be ridiculous," she mumbled.

"I'm not the one who's being ridiculous. You feel it, too. I know you do."

"I... I don't know what you mean."

He leaned forward, touched her cheek and chin, lifting her head so that once more their eyes met. "Liar."

"Just because you're a good kisser——"

He laughed. "Thank you very much."

"It wasn't a compliment. It was a statement of fact. I mean... Oh, heavens..." Her face was flaming.

"What are you afraid of?" MacPherson asked after a moment. "I mean, a woman like you——"

Her head jerked up. "What do you know about a woman like me?"

He opened his mouth, then stopped. His gaze, which had been challenging, became oddly assessing, slightly curious. The blue eyes were not quite so cold.

Emily stared at him, defiantly.

He looked down at the toes of his shoes, then back at her. "Maybe not as much as I thought I did."

She won the battle, not the war.

Tom hollered from the bathroom. MacPherson went to find him a towel. While he was gone, Emily breathed more easily. When he came back, she would ask him if she could use the phone to call Guido.

"Why?" he asked when she did.

"So he'll come and get me."

"And you don't think your friend will think to check?"

"I——"

"Come on, Emily. What are you afraid of? Me? Yourself?"

"Of course not!"

"Then...?"

"It's not a good idea."

"But you don't have a better one. You wouldn't want me to think badly of you, would you? Maybe look up your friend Gomez after you've left me..."

"You wouldn't!"

One dark brow lifted slightly. "How do you know what I'll do?"

"If you think for one minute I'll let you——"

"So stop me."

She blinked.

"Come with me to Chamonix."

Trapped. She should have seen it coming. Oh, Emily, you are so disgustingly naive. "I . . . I don't know if Tom will want to."

MacPherson smiled. "We'll ask him."

And that, Emily knew, meant that they would be going to Chamonix.

CHAPTER FOUR

THE day continued with the same aura of unreality with which it had begun.

Emily supposed that was because everything that was happening was so unexpected. She had thought she would be spending the day with Guido, catching up on old times, explaining about Tom, about Gomez, trying to make Guido understand what she was up to and why.

She ate and slept. Then ate again and slept some more.

MacPherson simply took over, and Emily let him.

No, that wasn't quite right. It was more that she couldn't stop him. He had a calm and logical answer for all her protests. He made her feel an idiot for making them.

And at the same time he made her feel cosseted and cared for. She hadn't felt like that in years. All the time she'd modeled, she'd rushed about to do someone else's bidding. With Marc, she'd always tried to please. And with Mari and Tom there was no question: she was needed, so she did what was expected of her. In this last, at least, there was no hardship. She did it out of love.

But no one had done it for her.

Until now.

"Rest," Mac had told her once they finished an enormous breakfast and he had shown her to her room. "Take a nap. I'll take care of Tom."

"But I——"

"You need a break. And Tom will be fine. Don't worry, I'll take care of him."

"You mustn't take him anywhere! Gomez might——"

"I can deal with Gomez." He didn't say how, but the tone in his voice left no doubt that he meant it.

And when he put his hand over hers, in spite of herself, she wanted to cling to it. Only because she was so tired, she thought. Only because she was at her wits' end. If she were rational, sensible, she'd run as fast as she could. But today, at least, Emily wasn't running anywhere.

"Come and lie down," he said, beckoning her toward the bedroom.

And Emily did as he said, letting him unbuckle her sandals and slip them off, watching as he drew back the duvet on the bed.

When he waited expectantly, she sat down, knotting her hands together, then looked up at him imploringly.

"You mustn't take him out."

"No farther than the garden," MacPherson promised, then smiled at her. "It's private. Only guests are allowed. Your dark-haired villain isn't a guest here, Emily. I guarantee it."

Emily looked at him mutely, still somewhat fearful, but he met her gaze steadily, determinedly. She swallowed, then nodded and bowed her head.

He squeezed her hand once more, then moved, and she felt something brush against the top of her hair, just barely touching her hair.

His hand? His *lips*?

Oh, heavens!

She looked up quickly. But he had turned away, out of the room, pulling the door shut behind him. She sat quite still for a few moments, trying to make sense of what the last eighteen hours had wrought, what a maelstrom of emotions she was experiencing. No order came from the chaos that was her mind, and so at last, confused and dazed, she had stripped off her dress and crawled under the duvet.

When she finally awoke, she knew she must have been asleep for a long time. The morning sun was gone. The room was in shadows now and the soft mutterings that had been MacPherson and Tom were silent.

She felt an instant's panic, then deliberately forced herself to relax. If something had gone awry, she would know. MacPherson would have come and told her.

Still, she got up quickly, washed her face and brushed her hair, then dressed in a pale pink T-shirt and blue cotton jumper, strapped on her sandals and went to look for them.

She didn't have to look far.

Tom was sound asleep on the small sofa, covered with a thin cotton blanket. The television was on, the volume low, but Mac was sitting at the desk, absorbed in a stack of papers.

He looked up when she opened the door. And the way he looked at her made her glance down hastily, as if she'd forgotten to put on her clothes.

He grinned, his expression knowing.

Emily lifted her chin. "Don't let me bother you," she said stiffly.

He stuck the papers in his briefcase and shut it, then shook his head. "No bother." He got to his feet and moved toward her.

She could see it again—that touch of the jungle cat—in his walk. He had a pantherish sort of grace, a sense of purpose. She could feel it, too, the sense of awareness, the almost electrical charge that seemed to arc between them.

Emily took a step back. She remembered his last touch. His lips? Her heart kicked over.

"Sleep well?" he asked her.

"Yes, thank you," she said quickly. "Has Tom been sleeping long?"

"An hour or so. We went out into the garden for a walk. And no, we didn't see your friend," he added when he saw the worried look on her face. "The concierge managed to come up with a toy boat that beat all the ones in Tom's bathtub fleet so we sailed it on the pond. Then we came back here, had a bit of lunch, then watched a football match. He nodded off. So I covered him up and managed at last to do a bit of work."

All the while he spoke he moved closer, until he stood scant inches from her. He lifted his hand and ran it over her hair.

Emily flinched away, swallowing. "I knew we'd disturb you."

"You disturb me, all right," he said, his voice husky with desire. "But it has nothing to do with work."

Emily gave her head a little shake and retreated to the far side of the room. "Don't. Please."

He followed her. "Why not?"

"Because... because we hardly know each other."

"We've spent the night together."

"Nothing happened!"

He lifted one dark brow. "Didn't it?" There was a wealth of meaning in his question—a challenge.

Emily's cheeks burned. Her fingers knotted together. "You know what I mean."

"I know. But not because we didn't want it. Isn't that true, Emily Musgrave?"

Helpless, Emily shook her head, trying to deny it.

"Ah, Emily." His grimace was wry. "Why can't you admit that much? I have." And the tone of his voice made Emily think he didn't like the admission any more than she did.

She gave him a curious look. But before she could pursue it, there was a movement from the sofa and Emily turned to see Tom stretching and opening his eyes. His gaze found first MacPherson, then Emily, and he smiled.

"We sailed a boat, Em. Did Mac tell you?" he asked eagerly, sitting up.

Mac. Emily winced. Tom had certainly been won over. "Was it fun?" She tried for interest, but not enthusiasm.

"The best. It was just like his, he said. His real one."

Emily looked at MacPherson. He seemed suddenly to be concentrating on the television screen. "I thought the concierge just happened to come up with a boat..."

He shrugged. "I told him what kind to look for."

"Mac says maybe some day I can sail on it," Tom told her eagerly.

The way he said Tom should learn to ride a pony? "Oh, he does, does he?" Emily said archly.

"Why not? You might be in Burnham-on-Crouch some day," MacPherson said gruffly. "You could come and see me."

"I thought you lived in London."

"Hertfordshire. But I keep my boat in Essex."

"I see."

"And the house in Spain is just outside Madrid. In case you're interested," he added, giving her a mocking smile.

Emily ignored him. "Why did you pick Spain?"

He looked at her blankly.

"I mean, why not France? Or Germany? I assume you were looking for a Continental base for the settings for your books."

"Oh, yeah, right." He shrugged. "I spent some holidays in Spain when I was a boy."

Emily tried to imagine him as a boy. Sometimes, when he grinned, she caught sight of a hint of the child he must have been. But the toughness of the man was far more obvious. He was a hard man, a determined man, and he looked it. Emily thought he looked every bit as dangerous as the spies he wrote about. She wondered if there was more than imagination in his books.

"Do you do a lot of research?" she asked him. "Or have you lived what you write?"

"You mean, do I break codes and sneak up on people?"

"Your books are more complicated than that," Emily protested.

He smiled. "Thanks. To answer your question, though, I guess you could say I daydream most, but it's grounded in reality. I have to base it on fact."

"Does that mean the next one will have something to do with sailing?" she asked.

"Yes. There's a bit of a chase, actually." He grinned, and she saw that gleam of boyish enthusiasm once more. It was as appealing as the rest of him. Dangerouser and dangerouser, she cautioned herself.

"Wow. You wrote about this boat?" Tom's eyes were wide. "An' I can go on it?"

"Sure," said MacPherson at the same time that Emily, realizing she was getting in deeper, said,

"I doubt we'll ever be in England."

"But if we are?"

"You didn't think you'd ever go to Chamonix either," MacPherson reminded her, and there was a light in his eyes again that invited further thoughts of the way she had felt at the touch of his lips, of the response he excited, of where that could lead.

Emily's fingers twisted more tightly.

"Well, Em?" Tom pressed.

"Well, Em?" Mac echoed softly, one dark brow lifted in challenge.

Oh, Emily, she asked herself, what are you getting into?

"We'll see."

All the way to Chamonix MacPherson was a perfect gentleman.

Of course, Emily thought wryly as she pressed her head against the glass and stared out of the window as the bus wound its way up the alpine valley, why shouldn't he be? He was getting his own way. He had commandeered her and charmed Tom. They were doing precisely what he suggested.

He'd called for a taxi bright and early this morning, and, with little fanfare, he'd whisked them off to the *gare routière*. Emily had kept an eagle eye out for Gomez, but she hadn't seen him anywhere.

"Probably still watching Guido's," MacPherson had said.

"Do you think so?" Emily considered calling Guido and asking, but it had been too early when they left. She'd do it later from Chamonix. Right now she listened to MacPherson continue to work his spell over young Tom.

She had protested when Tom had plopped down next to the window and looked up imploringly at Mac, asking, "Will you sit next to me?"

"You needn't be bothered with him all the time," she'd said.

"It's no bother," MacPherson had protested.

And Emily had to admit that it didn't seem to be. He was, in fact, every bit as good with Tom as she could have wished. Strong. Caring. Fatherly, almost. Exactly what Tom needed.

Once more she told herself that when she got back to the States she would have to set about meeting a few men, trying to find a permanent man in her life, trying to find a father for Tom.

Clearly she'd recovered from Marc, she thought ruefully. At least she had if her reactions to MacPherson were anything to go by!

She watched his dark head now as he leaned toward Tom and tried to sort out her reactions to him. She was attracted, there was no doubt about that. But what point was there? She wasn't a woman for one-night stands. She wanted true love, lasting love. She'd always envied David his unswerving conviction that Mari was his one and only. She'd hoped for a similar experience herself.

After what had happened with Marc, feeling sure that the rush of excitement and romance was just that and discovering her error, she'd grown skeptical and extremely cautious. At least she'd thought she had. Maybe, she realized now, she hadn't met a man since who'd stirred her interest.

MacPherson did. What was it about him that was different from all the other men who'd come into her life before and after Marc? Well, he was more attractive than most, that was certain. He wasn't pretty-boy gorgeous like some of the men she'd modeled with. But he had a sense of himself, an air about him that suggested he knew exactly who he was and what he wanted out of life. And he looked like a man who got what he wanted, too.

But there was more than power, more than strength. There had also been a hint of gentle caring that attracted Emily, too. It was so unexpected that it had caught her unawares. But it intrigued her, made her want to know more about what made him the way he was—a perplexing combination of toughness and tenderness.

There was, too, the fact that he hadn't tried to share her bed.

Of course she'd shared her room with Tom. But MacPherson had never suggested that she not, had never pressured her to leave her nephew and come to him. And it wasn't because he wasn't interested, either. Emily knew enough about men to know when they were interested in her. MacPherson was interested. His looks, his words had told her as much.

But he wasn't pushing.

Like now. He seemed quite content to sit next to Tom. She listened now as he told the boy something about glaciers. They'd been talking nonstop since breakfast—all about alpine skiing and mountain climbing and parapenting. It was evident, from Tom's eager questions, that her nephew felt he was embarking on the holiday of his dreams.

She wanted to lean forward and insert a voice of reason. She wanted to caution Tom about expecting too much. MacPherson was offering them a hideout, a few days' respite, not a lifetime of adventure. She hoped Tom realized that.

You'd never know it from the conversation, Emily thought wearily. They seemed to have more potential plans than the Alps had peaks. Now they were talking about going to the top of the Aiguille du Midi on the *télephérique*.

The thought made her shudder. She'd done a photo shoot once in the Italian Alps. She'd done her best, smiling gamely out of the window of the Italian version of the *télephérique*, thanking heaven and the photographer all the while that it never really went anywhere, just hovered, for the photographer's convenience, about twenty feet above the ground.

The notion of actually boarding one of those cable cars and being hoisted through midair to the tip of a cloud-ridden peak made Emily's stomach lurch.

"Have you gone up there?" Tom wanted to know. "Is it scary?"

MacPherson shook his head. "Not unless you run into a thunderstorm."

Emily cringed.

"Have you parapented? Climbed? Skied?"

"All of the above."

"Can I?"

"You can go up in the *télephérique*," Mac replied. "And maybe we can do a bit of climbing. The skiing isn't good this late in the year, and no, you can't parapent. Your aunt would have my head."

This last, spoken in a carrying voice, was for Emily's benefit. And she could tell from the sound of his voice that he was smiling as he said it.

Tom giggled and turned to pop his head over the back of the seat. "Wouldn't you like to parapent, Em?"

"Jump off the tops of mountains in a parachute? No, thank you very much. I'm not that brave."

Mac turned his head and their eyes met. Emily felt that now familiar jolt of awareness. "On the contrary," he said quite seriously after a moment, "I'd say you're very brave indeed."

Because she was standing up to Gomez? she wondered. Because she'd come to Chamonix with him? Emily wasn't sure which he meant. She only knew that the intensity of his gaze embarrassed her. "I do what I have to," she mumbled.

MacPherson's gaze met hers steadily. "So do I."

And Emily subsided into silence, wondering, as well, what he meant by that.

Their trip to Chamonix brought them back into France again. And when Emily descended from the bus she was charmed at the small bustling town nestled against the snow-covered alpine peaks.

In winter, she imagined, the pace would be considerably more frenetic. As it was small groups of people milled about, taking photos, checking the large city map, ambling down the street toward the shops and restaurants that beckoned.

Emily herself moved slowly, carefully, taking a thorough look around to confirm what she'd been hoping since they'd boarded the bus that morning—Gomez was nowhere to be seen. When she had, she allowed herself a deep breath of pure mountain air and smiled a smile of pure bliss.

MacPherson smiled, too. "Told you so. Now relax. Come on." He took her hand in his. "We'll get a taxi to my apartment."

His apartment was right across the Arve River in a three-story stucco and timber building set back from the street and overlooking the fast-moving river which tumbled along behind it.

MacPherson unlocked the door and held it open, ushering them into a tiled hallway with stairs leading upward on the right. "No elevator—sorry," he said. "I'm clear at the top."

Tom led the way, bounding eagerly ahead. MacPherson followed him and Emily brought up the rear. Off the stairs on the first floor there were two doors. At the top there was only one.

"The penthouse?" Emily asked dryly.

"In a manner of speaking." He turned the key in the lock and pushed open the door, letting them in a small entryway that opened on to a sunlit, but stuffy, living room.

Tall windows directly faced the river and, beyond it, the Mont Blanc mountain range. MacPherson crossed the room and opened the windows, letting the breeze and the sound of the river fill the room. The wind caught the curtain and blew it back, and Emily's breath caught at the stunning view.

"Two bedrooms over here." Mac moved to the far end of the room and opened first one door and then the other. He slanted her a grin. "Want to share with me or Tom?"

"How about you and Tom sharing," Emily said impulsively, "and I'll have one of my own?"

Mac shrugged. "Fair enough." He picked up his and Tom's duffels and headed toward one of the bedrooms.

"I was just kidding," Emily said hastily.

"I don't mind."

"I'd like it," Tom said flatly.

"But——"

MacPherson turned to Tom. "Why don't you unpack your gear into the bureau on the far side?" And when Tom went to do just that, Mac turned to Emily. "Let him share with me. You can't hover over him forever."

"I'm not hovering."

"Looks to me like you are. He's a boy, not a baby. He needs a bit of space."

"I know!"

"Well, then?" He gave her an arch look.

"I just... don't want him to bother you."

"I'm a big boy, too. I can defend myself. How about if I assure you that I won't let him bother me. If I begin to find him obnoxious and unpleasant I'll pitch him right out on his ear."

"He's not obnoxious!"

MacPherson grinned. "My point exactly."

Emily fumed under her breath.

"So, are we in agreement? If I invite him to do something, or if I say I don't mind if he does something, you will not jump in to protect me."

"I don't protect you!"

"You try."

"I don't want him to be a pest. I don't want either one of us to bother you. I——"

He shook his head, his expression almost rueful. "Emily, Emily. It's all right. Relax. You're taking this far too seriously."

"It is serious."

A corner of his mouth quirked. "You amaze me," he said softly. "I never figured..." He shook his head once again.

"Never figured what?" Emily demanded.

"That you'd be so...so...conscientious."

"Of course I'm conscientious. I'm Tom's guardian!"

"But you're going to make yourself ill if you keep worrying about every little thing."

"I have to," Emily insisted.

"Do you? Is it Tom you're worried about, Emily? Or yourself?"

"*What*?" She looked at him, horrified.

"Is that why you want him in with you? As a shield?"

"Oh, for heaven's sake!" Emily turned away, hugging her arms against her breasts.

"First I thought you were a fickle witch," MacPherson said softly. "And for just a bit I thought you were an ice princess. But you're not, are you, Emily? You're just scared." His voice was caressing almost, belying the challenge in his words.

"You're dreaming," Emily said tersely.

"Am I?" He smiled. "I wonder."

"All right," she said gruffly. "He can stay in your room. For tonight."

"And we can keep the door open between the two rooms."

Emily looked at him, startled. "But——"

He laughed. "I thought you were worried about Tom."

"Well, I—"

"Did I jump your bones last night? Or the night before?"

"No, but..."

He winked. "I told you, I'm a big boy, Emily. I can wait."

"I can wait."

The words echoed in her ears. They had been spoken so matter-of-factly, so bluntly. No "ifs" or "maybes." Just "I can wait." As if it was inevitable.

Was it?

Emily found herself trembling at the thought. What had she got herself into—coming to Chamonix with him, moving into his apartment?

What was she doing not rejecting the idea out of hand? This wasn't like her. Yet, she had to acknowledge, MacPherson didn't make her feel like herself.

He was like Marc, she tried telling herself, bowling her over, making her crazy. And of course, Marc had. But Marc had wanted her simply as a showpiece in his collection. He had wanted to possess her. Even when she'd repulsed his advances he'd persisted in his desire to marry her. But not, as she had hoped, because he honored her principles; only because he was making real love to someone else.

MacPherson had said nothing about marriage, of course. He was talking about sex, pure and simple. She ought to be running away as fast as she could!

And why wasn't she? she asked herself.

Gomez, she thought at once. But she'd eluded Gomez now. He wasn't the reason she was hanging around now.

So what was?

The answer was harder to come by than she'd thought. Attraction? Well, yes. Curiosity? That, too. Hope for the future? That didn't seem very likely. They'd scarcely known each other two days. But there was something in the way he looked at her. Something warm and possessive, something strong and protective? Was she dreaming?

"Don't get your hopes up," she told herself.

Heavens, she thought, she didn't even know if he was married.

She assumed he wasn't. Certainly he didn't act married.

But what did that mean? For a year she hadn't thought Howell was married, either. If he hadn't casually mentioned his daughter, she might have gone on even longer. Even then she'd assumed he was divorced until one day Howell had said, "Bad idea, divorce. Creates too many off-shoot families. Kids get torn."

"Did yours?" Emily had asked, and Howell had looked at her, astonished.

"I'm not divorced. Sian and I have been married twenty-four years."

"But I've never met her."

Howell had shrugged. "She doesn't live in my pocket. She does her thing. I do mine."

Emily didn't understand, but she hadn't argued with him.

Later, when she'd run to him after the fiasco with Marc, she'd cringed at the rumors she'd spawned, worried about what they'd do to his marriage. "Howell Evans's New Bimbo", one headline had read. And "Sian's Fed Up," blared another.

But as far as Emily knew Sian Evans went right on sculpting as she always had, oblivious to Howell's supposed transgression. And if, when she'd had a highly touted show in London a few months later, Howell didn't go, Emily had learned it wasn't because they were on the outs, though the papers claimed that. She didn't want him there, Howell had explained.

"It's her baby, not mine," he'd told Emily when she'd called him, worried still. "If I'm there people ask me about my photos, they try to compare us. There is no comparison. I told you, we each do our own thing. Quit fussing."

Emily had.

Keeping Howell in mind, she thought she'd better learn a bit more about MacPherson. There was no sense in making a fool of herself over him.

She looked around MacPherson's apartment for signs of feminine habitation, expecting that even if he had a wife who did her own thing she might deign to go skiing with him. But though there were a few feminine toiletries in the bathroom there were no women's clothes in the bureau, no dresses in the wardrobe.

"Looking for something?" MacPherson asked when he walked in to find her staring at the empty cabinet.

"Your wife."

He laughed. "Good luck."

"I mean, I don't even know if you're married!"

"I'm not. Yet." He grinned. "Want to ask me anything else?"

There were a million things Emily would have liked to have asked. She shook her head. "Not at all."

After they were unpacked and settled in, Mac suggested a stroll around town to get a meal and buy groceries. And taking her arm, he steered her, open-mouthed, down the stairs and out into the street. Tom skipped eagerly along after them.

The air was crisp and cool in the shade even in mid June. But the direct sun was warming, and Emily stopped in the middle of the small garden to sigh and stretch in the heat of its rays.

She felt fingertips on her nape, lightly massaging. She stiffened for an instant, then melted. Protest died on her lips. She sighed. Smiled. Shut her eyes.

"C'mon, Em," Tom shouted from the road.

She opened her eyes again to find MacPherson's face very close. His cool blue eyes looked surprisingly warm, as if there were a flicker of firelight deep within them.

She swallowed.

He smiled, then dropped his hand to take hers in his. "Come along. Let's do some exploring."

Chamonix was a paradise for boys, big and little, with umpteen mountaineering shops which drew both Mac and Tom like magnets. Food was forgotten as they prowled through reel after reel of climbing rope, pulling and testing, then moved on to look at climbing shoes, harnesses, pitons, axes and carabiners. From the mountaineering stores they moved to the sporting goods stores, the bike shops and the ski shops.

"Oooh, look," Tom would say when they'd left one to come face-to-face with another even more tempting.

"Just one more," MacPherson promised time after time.

Emily didn't care. She might not know a carabiner from a catfish, but she was perfectly content to while away the time looking at sportswear and postcards and souvenir cowbells. It was calming just to be able to move about without looking over her shoulder, comforting to hear Tom's eager chatter and see the smile on his face.

It was a respite. But as she sat on a bench in the sunshine and watched through the window as MacPherson hunkered down to Tom's level, showing him how to tie some sort of knot, then holding the boy's hands and helping him go through the motions until he could do it himself, she found herself wishing it could be more.

When they emerged, they had a coil of rope which Tom carried in his arms as if it were a baby. He was grinning from ear to ear.

"Look, Em!" He showed it off proudly. "We're gonna climb."

"Hike," MacPherson corrected before she could say a word.

She looked at him skeptically. "You need a rope to hike?"

"Some of the trails are a bit steep. It's a precautionary measure. A tether, if you like. We thought we'd hike down from the first station of the *téléphérique*."

Emily looked at the high, jagged snow-covered peaks, at the tiny red dot moving slowly down the cable at an angle to the rock face. Steep wasn't the word she'd have used to describe it. Her stomach felt queasy just looking at it.

Her trepidation must have showed, for Mac grinned at her. "You're not chicken, are you, Miss Musgrave?"

She lifted her chin. "Of course not."

He laughed.

They found an outdoor café overlooking the Arve which served a mixed grill lunch. Tom shared his seat with the coil of rope and hugged it at every chance he got. The moment he'd finished eating he pleaded to go up that very afternoon.

"Not today," Mac said. "We want good weather."

"It's sunny," Tom protested.

"Now. But the wind will come up later and the clouds will come in." Mac squinted upward. "We might even get a bit of rain."

Emily looked at him, astonished, for the clouds, as far as she could see, were almost nonexistent. But she certainly wasn't going to disagree with him. She remembered what he'd said about being stuck in a thunderstorm.

"We'll go tomorrow morning when the weather's clear."

Tom looked as if he was going to argue further, but MacPherson fixed him with a firm look. "Tomorrow."

"Can I go watch the river, then?"

Emily nodded and watched him go. He looked bright and happy today, the way she wanted him to look, the way he hadn't looked in months.

She wondered if Alejandro Gomez would be pleased to know he'd accomplished so much on his nephew's behalf. The thought made her smile.

"What's funny?"

"I was just thinking about Gomez."

"He makes you smile?"

"Not usually. Usually he makes me angry."

MacPherson took a swallow of beer. "Do you really think he's that much of an ogre?"

"He certainly was to his sister. He kidnapped her."

"What!"

"Well, maybe technically he didn't, but it amounted to the same thing. The family didn't want her dating David. My brother. She was supposed to marry the man Papa picked out for her."

"That's not unheard-of."

"Maybe not," Emily conceded grudgingly. "But they were so determined. So rigid. They wouldn't even listen. When Marielena said she didn't want to marry their choice, the Gomezes didn't take no for an answer. They told her if she married David they'd disown her! And when she said she was going to marry David anyway, clever Alejandro tried to stop her from showing up at the wedding."

"Maybe he just wanted to plead his case."

Emily scowled. "Whose side are you on?"

"Yours, of course. But——"

"What would you call spiriting her away the night before the wedding, taking her way off to some god-forsaken country house and trying to browbeat her all night?"

"Obviously he didn't do any good."

"Of course not! She loved David. She told Gomez he didn't know anything about love. And he agreed with her!" Emily shook her head just the way she had when Marielena had told her about it years ago. "Boy, is that the truth!"

She turned and watched Tom again. He was tossing pebbles into the river, hopping on first one foot, then the other.

"So what happened?" MacPherson asked finally.

"He finally saw that he couldn't change her mind. Anyway, she showed up at the ceremony flaming mad moments before it was going to begin. David was a nervous wreck. I know he thought she'd changed her mind, that the family had convinced her, but she said she never wanted to see them again. I know David felt bad that she and her brother hadn't reconciled, but you never saw anyone so relieved when she finally got there."

In her mind's eye Emily could still see her brother's anxious face, then the heart-stopping smile that had appeared when Marielena had come in the door. She smiled at the memory. "I was so happy for both of them. They were so much in love. You could just see it on their faces. If Alejandro Gomez had bothered to look, he might have seen it too."

MacPherson drained his glass of beer and set it on the table. His finger traced a circle in the condensation. "And they lived happily ever after, did they?"

"They had four years. Four good years." She swallowed against the tightness in her throat. "And they had Tom. Yes, I think you could say they did."

MacPherson's gaze followed her own. They watched as Tom hung over the railing, dropping pebbles, his dark hair whipped in the breeze. "He's a very special little boy," he said at last.

"He is. I'd die if I had to let him go. I *won't* let him go."

"No," MacPherson said quietly. "I don't expect you will."

CHAPTER FIVE

IT WAS all very well to agree with MacPherson that Tom should spend the night with him. It was something else again to sit at the dressing table brushing her hair in the next room and listen to the sound of Tom's high-pitched voice, then Mac's lower-pitched rumble. They were laughing, then talking some more, like old friends, bosom buddies. She wondered what they were talking about.

Tom used to talk at length to anyone who would listen. But in the last few months, since his mother's death, he'd become much quieter.

Except today with MacPherson. Today he'd been the old Tom, chattering a mile a minute, bounding ahead, then running back to share some titbit of information, some fascinating idea he'd just thought of. And every other word seemed to have been "Mac."

"Mr. MacPherson," Emily had tried belatedly to insist upon. MacPherson had rolled his eyes.

Tom had simply said, "He likes me callin' him Mac." Emily could see that making an issue of it would never work.

"Just don't get your hopes up, little one," she whispered now, hearing over the running water a high-pitched giggle and Tom's exaggerated, "Oh, Mac!"

Then, all of a sudden, the door to her room flew open and Tom hurtled through.

He was ready for bed, hair damp, face scrubbed, and he flung himself on her, a grin on his face. "I came to kiss you good-night," he announced.

She looked up to see MacPherson right behind him.

Emily dropped her brush and caught Tom to her, using his wriggling six-year-old body to cover as much of her as her skimpy nightgown did not.

Logically she knew that if Mac had seen her on the cover of half a dozen magazines he had certainly seen more of her than she was showing now. But it wasn't the same. Those were posed, impersonal, two-dimensional, and, as far as Emily was concerned, not really *her*. This was.

She gave Tom a quick smacking kiss. "Good night," she said, curling her long bare legs under the cotton of her nightgown.

Mac watched, grinning. "Do I get a good-night kiss too?"

Emily made a face at him, but Tom beamed. "Yeah," he chimed in. "Mac, too."

"Tom! For goodness' sake!"

"You always made me kiss Gloria."

"Gloria is a friend. It's not the same thing."

"Mac is a friend, too, you said so," Tom reminded. "An' he doesn't smell like paint thinner."

MacPherson winced. "A backhanded compliment, I think." Still, he didn't seem averse to capitalizing on it. He tapped a spot on his cheek and grinned at Emily. "Just a small one. Right here. I won't tax your strength."

"You kissed him at the train station," Tom reminded her.

"That was different."

Tom looked at her, wide-eyed. "Oh? How?"

Explanations, Emily knew from experience, would do no good at all. She might just as well kiss him and get it over with.

Besides, there was a certain truth to the old quotation about "protesting too much." "Fine." She set Tom on the floor, got up, still keeping as much of herself covered as possible, and pecked MacPherson on the cheek.

"There." She gave a brisk nod. "Satisfied."

"Yup." Tom beamed.

"Not a chance," Mac murmured. He took Tom by the shoulders and steered him toward his room. "But I guess it'll have to do. For now." And with a wink over his shoulder, he chivvied Tom out of the room.

Emily sank down on the bed again, her lips still tingling from the brief contact with Mac's faintly bristly cheek. Get control of yourself, she mentally admonished. But it took more than one deep breath to restore her equilibrium.

"He's not that handsome," she muttered to herself.

But handsome wasn't the issue. He attracted her. He was strong and capable, yet solicitous and kind, sexy yet caring. A lethal combination. But would it go anywhere?

She didn't know.

Mac hadn't shut the door when he and Tom left, and Emily got up to shut it now. She paused, doing so, caught by the conversation.

"You really think we can hike tomorrow?" Tom was asking.

"If the weather's good."

There was a slight pause. Then, "I'm glad," Tom said. "I didn't think I'd ever get to go hiking. I thought you needed a dad for that."

Emily's breath caught in her throat.

"You were very little when he died, weren't you?" she heard Mac ask him.

"Three. I 'member some things. He used to ride me on his shoulders. And sometimes on the weekends we'd go out and buy the newspaper and a *coca* and bring them back and crawl into bed again with Mommy." Tom's voice wavered a little. "They'd read the paper and we'd all eat the *coca* and drink coffee, and tell jokes and laugh."

"You must miss him a lot."

"Yeah." Tom's voice was a bare whisper. "I want him back. I want my mom back, too."

There was a long moment of silence, then the sound of a sob, followed by another. Emily started to open the door, then heard Mac move.

"Come here," he said and she heard a shuffling noise and then what sounded like the sobs being muffled into his shirt.

"Oh, hell, Tom," he muttered. "Oh, God, I'm sorry."

Emily froze, her hand on the door handle. She should go in, take Tom in her arms and comfort him. Right after his mother's death, he'd sobbed and sobbed. But over the past couple of months he'd come out of it, looking forward, not back. And Emily had felt he was getting over it.

Now she felt as if no time had passed at all. She thought she should intervene, yet wondered about the wisdom of it. He hadn't confided this to her, but to Mac.

More muffled sniffles, then she heard, "'S'okay. 'M Okay," and Mac promising,

"You will be. I swear it."

Tom hiccuped. "I don' usually cry," he mumbled.

"It's all right to cry."

There was a pause. "Do you? Sometimes?" Tom's voice was still a little croaky.

Emily waited, as curious as Tom. She couldn't imagine Sandy MacPherson crying.

"Yes."

"Did you when your parents died?" Tom asked him.

"I did when my father died. My mother's still alive. But she has a bad heart."

"Is she gonna die?"

"I hope not. It worries me."

"Yeah," Tom said after a moment, and Emily knew he was remembering his own worries, settling down now that he realized they weren't unique. "I know what you mean. Do you got brothers and sisters?"

There was a pause. Then, Mac said quietly, "No. I don't have anyone but my mother now."

"I'm lucky. I've got Emily. I wouldn't have nobody if I didn't have Emily."

Emily felt her cheeks heat and was conscious once more of eavesdropping. Still she couldn't move away.

"What about your mother's family?" she heard Mac ask.

"They don't like me."

"What do you mean, they don't like you?" Mac sounded offended.

"They didn't like my daddy. They didn't want my mommy to marry him."

"How do you know that?"

"My mommy said so."

There was a long silence. Emily felt, if not pleased, at least vindicated. If Mac had thought she was exaggerating about the lack of rapport between the Gomez family and her brother and sister-in-law, he would know now that she wasn't the only one to feel that way.

"I think they were pretty dumb, don't you?" Tom said candidly.

"Yes," Emily heard MacPherson reply, "yes, I do." There was a pause. Then, "Here. Blow." Emily heard Tom give a mighty blow of his nose. "Better?" Mac asked.

"Uh-huh."

"Time for lights-out, then."

"Emily always reads me a story."

"Want me to call her?"

"Not tonight," Tom said matter-of-factly. "She'll see I been crying and she'll be sad. I don't want Emily to be sad. So, will you? Read it, I mean?"

"If you're sure..."

Was that hesitation in MacPherson's voice?

"You know how, don't you?" Tom sounded momentarily worried.

MacPherson laughed. "I write 'em, remember?"

"That's right. I'll get it out of my bag." Emily heard him bounce down onto the floor and cross the room, rummage through his duffel and come back. "I'm glad you're Emily's friend, Mac," he said as he bounced back to the bed, making the springs creak. "I like you."

And before she eased the door completely shut and tiptoed back to her bed, Emily heard Mac say softly, "I like you, too."

The morning dawned bright and still. A perfect day to go to the Aiguille du Midi, according to Mac. As far as Emily was concerned, no day was perfect to dangle so far above the world in what seemed to her a very tiny cable-car compartment.

"You don't have to come if you don't want to," Mac said. "I can take him by myself."

"No." She shook her head, adamant. "I'm going. I need to."

Emily couldn't have said precisely why she felt so strongly about it. It wasn't as if she feared that Alejandro Gomez was going to be waiting at the top of the Aiguille du Midi, ready to snatch Tom out of Mac's grasp and she had to be there to prevent it. But it did have something to do with Gomez, something to do with what she'd overheard last night between Mac and Tom, something to do with Tom's protecting her.

It should be the other way around, she'd thought then. She should be protecting and caring for Tom. That was what this flight into France was all about. So Gomez would forget them and they could live in peace together.

But obviously he didn't intend to forget them. He had pursued them to Geneva. If he'd momentarily lost them, it only meant that his physical pursuit had been stymied. He still had legal recourse, or he must think he did.

There would be a fight now, Emily knew that for certain. Emily didn't like confrontations. She didn't like battles. But if caring for Tom meant a battle, she'd do it. So she needed to start facing her fears, and conquering them.

She was starting this morning by going up in the *téléphérique*.

They had to wait nearly an hour until their number was called to board the cable car. The whole while Emily watched nervously as the small red cars lurched up out of the station and edged their way up the face of the mountain.

"You sure about this?" Mac asked in her ear as she stood, chewing the inside of her cheek and mentally distributing her worldly goods.

She ventured a fleeting smile. "I'll be fine. It's just nerves."

All the same she was grateful he was there to keep an eye on Tom, because she was hardly capable of doing it. It was all she could do, when the time came, to allow herself to be herded through the station and into the waiting car where she stood pressed against a window, one hand gripping one of the uprights, her eyes fixed on the mountain ahead.

She felt strong fingers lace through hers and Mac's shoulder hard against her own. "I've got an idea," he whispered in her ear, and she could hear the smile in his voice. The cable car lurched and began its ascent.

"What's that?" Emily managed, but her voice cracked.

"You need to take your mind off it. Think about something more important."

What, Emily wondered, could be more important than concentrating every single thought on making sure the cable didn't break?

"This." And Mac's warm lips closed over hers, a firm arm came around her, pulling her hard against a strong body.

It could have been the altitude, or her fear of heights, or any number of things. But whatever it was, Emily's world shrank, her ears rang, and her gasp for breath was cut short.

Her hand loosed the upright and came to clutch his jacket, her fingers curling into the soft cotton as she clung to him desperately, lost in the heady warmth and hunger of his touch.

"You're missin' the best part," Tom complained at her elbow.

No, Emily thought. Not true. Nothing in the world could be better than this.

The impatient unrelenting shoving at her back was her first indication that the earth had stopped moving. Her earth hadn't.

But a cleared throat, a muttered, "*Pardon, mademoiselle*," followed by a definite jostle as the door opened, brought her back to reality.

Blushing she stammered, "*Oui, monsieur. Pardon.*" And still gripped in Mac's embrace, she was shuffled off the cable car and on to another.

"Wha——?" she began.

But the kiss began again, taking up right where it had left off.

"Ma—mmmm." Her protest was swallowed by his lips. She heard titters, she heard murmurings. She didn't care. She cared only for MacPherson.

It was only when the cable car jolted once more and the pushing and muttering began again and MacPherson took a small step back and allowed a millimeter of space between their lips that she breathed again.

"Maybe that wasn't such a great idea." His voice was hoarse, and she noticed for the first time the tide of color that had crept into his face and the telltale pulse hammering in his temple.

"It got me up here," she said in a voice only slightly more shaky than his.

MacPherson looked around them at the crowd, at the walkway that spanned the gorge between two parts of the peak. "Swell," he muttered. "Rather it'd got you into bed."

Emily, feeling as safe as ever she was likely to at three thousand, eight hundred and forty-two meters, grinned at him. "You're quite a Boy Scout."

"Aren't I, though?" he said wryly.

"Can we go to the top, Mac? Can we?" Tom pestered.

"To the top?" Emily echoed faintly. "What for pity's sake is this?"

"Close," Tom said and pointed toward the elevator that would take them even higher.

"Why not?" Mac said wryly. "We've come this far."

Emily, refusing to look down, allowed Mac to steer her across the bridge that spanned the crevasse between the building housing the *téléphérique* station and a restaurant-cum-gift shop and the topmost point where Tom was headed. At least she was upright and functioning.

In this instance she would take her victories where she could find them.

They lined up for the elevator, then were ushered in, packed like sardines and the doors closed. The elevator began to rise. Ordinarily elevators were not a problem.

It must have been the altitude, she thought afterward. Or the claustrophobic sensation of sharing a cramped space with eleven other people. She didn't know what else could have possessed her to croak, "I could use another kiss."

MacPherson stared at her. "Is this torment or is this torment?"

"If I have to suffer, you do, too."

"What a way to go," he groaned, and once more his lips closed over hers.

It was amazing how well it worked.

"My dad and mom used to kiss like that. Maybe you two should get married," Tom said.

That and the sudden stop of the elevator brought Emily back to reality with a thump. She pulled back, mortified, her hand going to her lips. "Tom!"

But MacPherson only smiled. "There's an idea."

Emily swallowed, staring at him.

He shrugged equably at her lack of response. "Ah, well. It was a thought."

He seemed as unfazed by the idea as Emily was stunned—not by the idea so much as by his apparent equanimity. Could he possibly be interested in more than a simple flirtation?

She pulled away from him and deliberately walked over to the edge of the platform, gripping the railing until the vertigo passed and she dared open her eyes to the panoramic vista before her.

The French Alps from above were even more dramatic than they were seen from below. There was a wildness to them, a grandeur, that Emily had never found in the mountains of her native America. The Rockies, daunting though they were, seemed tame by comparison.

And, as long as she didn't look straight down at mountaineers no bigger than pinpricks picking their way along a snow- and ice-covered trail, she could handle it, even marvel at the beauty of it.

It was, in fact, she thought, easier to handle than the heady notion of marrying MacPherson. Why hadn't he rejected it? Why had he looked at her with the speculative look in his eye?

"Glad you came after all?" Mac's voice said in her ear, startling her.

"It was worth the trip," she said without thinking.

"Thank you. I think," he added wryly, and Emily, remembering suddenly just what she had spent the trip doing, laughed and blushed again.

"Don't do that," he said.

"Do what?"

"Blush. It plays havoc with my hormones."

"It's the altitude."

He smiled. "That's what you think."

They spent another half hour on the top, and Emily didn't know which made her giddier, the altitude or the look in MacPherson's eyes. She was glad when they took the elevator down and stopped in the restaurant and gift shop where Tom bought a patch of the Aiguille du Midi for Emily to sew on his jacket and Mac bought them ham sandwiches and hot chocolate.

"A man can't live on kisses alone," he said in Emily's ear.

She flushed and gave him a little push, and he grinned. "You're doing it again. Blushing."

"Where're we gonna sit?" Tom demanded. "All the tables are taken."

"Sit here, sweetie," said a distinctly American voice. A sixtyish woman patted a place at the long Formica table she was sharing with three other women.

Tom looked at Emily, who nodded. "Thank you very much," she said, slipping into a seat next to the woman, pointing Tom to the chair across the table. Mac, carrying the tray of drinks and sandwiches sat down next to him.

"I'm Maggie Copeland from Dallas."

"Emily Musgrave," Emily said, because the woman was obviously expecting a response.

"I'm Tom," Tom said through a huge bite of his sandwich.

Maggie Copeland smiled at him. "So nice to see families here," she said to Emily. "Can't understand families who leave their kids at home and go gallivanting all over the world without 'em. Walter and I used to take ours everywhere, open their eyes, let them see the world. Glad to see you agree."

Emily nodded, her mouth full.

"Definitely," MacPherson said. Emily shot him a look of consternation.

Maggie beamed. "You sound British, but your wife sounds as if she's from the States."

"She is," MacPherson said while Emily made strangling noises.

Maggie Copeland looked again at Tom. "Just the one little boy?"

"For the moment." MacPherson gave Maggie Copeland a devilish wink.

All the women at the table let out a chorus of appreciative cackles. Emily choked on her sandwich.

Maggie reached over and patted her hand. "Be glad he's still so interested, dear," she counseled. "So many husbands are busy looking the other way."

Emily swallowed. At last. "He's not——"

"Of course he's not," Maggie said emphatically. "Nor is he ever likely to. My Walter was just the same. The marrying kind. The faithful kind. You can see it in their eyes."

Emily would have loved to look into MacPherson's eyes at that moment, desperate to know just what exactly it was that Maggie saw there. But there was no way she could bring herself to do it. She buried her face in her cup of hot chocolate.

"Must go. Come along, girls," Maggie pushed her chair back. She gave Emily's shoulder a squeeze. "All the best to you. And I must say, I hope you have half a dozen more." She paused and gave Tom another look, then turned back to Emily. "You two make handsome kiddies."

It was a full minute before Emily could bring herself to look at MacPherson. When she did, he was grinning like the Cheshire cat. "You could have corrected her," she said accusingly.

"Why? She would have been disappointed and embarrassed if she'd found out otherwise after making her assumptions. Besides, did you really want to explain everything to her?"

"No, of course not."

"Well, then . . . ?"

Emily sighed. She couldn't explain it without sounding like an idiot. How did you say to a man that you had been entertaining such thoughts yourself, that the idea was surprisingly tempting? "It made me uncomfortable," she said finally.

"What did? The idea of being married? Or being married to me?"

"Don't be silly."

"I'm not." He shifted in his chair, his mouth curving into a hint of a smile. "Tom suggested it, if you recall."

"Tom's a child! Children say all sorts of silly things."

"Did you think it was silly?"

"I..." She wished she hadn't finished her sandwich so quickly. She would have loved to have her mouth full right now.

"Just for the record, do you plan to get married some day?"

"Of course, when the right man comes along."

"What if he already has?"

The altitude was making her ears ring, making her hear words she didn't believe she could possibly have heard. She swallowed desperately, trying to clear her ears, trying to make sense of the words she thought he'd just said. What if he already had? Did that mean...?

"I—I...haven't considered it," she lied.

"Consider it, then." He pushed back his chair and stood up. "And let me know. Ready to go?" he asked Tom, who had been watching as another little boy shredded his lunch on to his plate.

"Can I look at those key chains over there first?"

"Why not?" Mac took his hand and started toward the counter, then stopped and looked back over his shoulder. "Take your time," he said to Emily, then smiled. "Enjoy your lunch."

CHAPTER SIX

ENJOY your lunch.

Consider marriage.

They probably weren't mutually exclusive notions, but you couldn't have proved it by Emily as she sat and stared after the man who had suggested them to her.

Surely he was kidding?

He had followed Tom to look at the souvenir key chains and was now hunkered down beside the boy so that their dark heads were level as they contemplated the display in the glass case. They were having a quiet conversation, all very ordinary, just as if he hadn't virtually proposed marriage to her five seconds before!

Or had he? Maybe she was deluding herself.

"You could marry me," Bob Duggan had said. And she hadn't had any trouble at all figuring out what he meant. She even knew he was quite serious.

But marry Sandy MacPherson? Certainly there was an attraction. But she couldn't imagine MacPherson hadn't been attracted to other women in his life. Surely he didn't propose to them all.

Emily tried to take a bite of her sandwich. She couldn't manage even a nibble. She felt as if she were trying to swallow Mont Blanc.

When she'd set off with Tom two days ago—was that all the time it had been? It seemed like years—it had been a simple proposition: outwit Alejandro Gomez, try to make him forget about her and go back to his own affairs or, failing that, win enough time and distance to get back to the States undetected where she could fight on her own turf.

In the meantime, she'd blithely promised herself, she and Tom would have a carefree holiday. Fat chance.

Marry MacPherson?

By rights, the idea ought to appall her. She'd shanghaied him into playing her husband, had actually *picked him up*, for pity's sake! But as she watched him smile now, then nod at something Tom said, and throw back his head and laugh, Emily felt her throat tighten, felt something deep inside her begin to ache.

Maggie Copeland was right: they could be mistaken for members of the same family if one didn't know they weren't. They both had straight dark hair and lean faces, although Tom had her brother David's wide brown eyes, innocent eyes, quite unlike the sea blue depths of MacPherson's. But Maggie Copeland had liked his eyes. She'd said they were like her husband's. Walter was, she'd said, a faithful man, a marrying man.

But was MacPherson?

What did Emily really know about him? Not much other than that he wrote bestselling spy novels, was peripatetic, handsome, good with children, and was an extremely fast worker.

Who in their right mind would consider marrying someone they knew so little? She should laugh. But she wasn't. Maybe, she thought, it was because she wasn't in her right mind. Maybe Gomez's pursuit was taking its toll.

He gave the cashier some money, and he and Tom were coming toward her. Hastily Emily drained her cup of cocoa. She couldn't have finished the sandwich if she'd been paid to.

"We got key chains just alike," Tom told her. "An" Mac got one for you." He handed her one with a picture of the *téléphérique* on it. "So you'll always remember today."

And looking at MacPherson, trying to divine the motivations behind those determined blue eyes, Emily wondered how she was ever supposed to forget.

"That was...very kind of him." Her fingers closed around the key chain. "Thank you."

His eyes smiled at her, and she saw the fiery flickering in their depths once more. "My pleasure."

"I wanted him to get the skier one, but he said no," Tom went on. "He said we were getting the *téléphérique*, that it was——" Tom screwed up his face as he tried to remember the word "—sig-nif-icant."

Tom looked at her for an explanation, but Emily didn't give him one, even though there was no doubt at all in her mind about what Mac meant. The man was serious. At least she thought he was.

Emily didn't ask him to kiss her on the way back down. He didn't suggest it. He did hold her hand tightly, and, while she was grateful for the grip of his strong fingers, she found herself wondering what it would be like to have those fingers to hold on to for the rest of her life.

She never once worried that the cable might break or the clouds overhead might split with lightning or that they might be suspended above the world forever. She had other, more important things to think about.

"You're unawakened," Howell always told her. "That's why I like photographing you. It's like seeing Sleeping Beauty before the kiss."

The fingers on Emily's other hand touched her mouth. She could still feel the tingle where MacPherson's lips had touched hers, as if they'd awakened her.

She wondered what Howell would think if he saw her

now. She was so preoccupied that she scarcely noticed when they jolted to a stop at the Plan and got out.

"Is this where we hike from?" Tom asked.

Emily looked up, startled. She'd forgotten.

"It's up to your aunt," MacPherson said.

"You go ahead."

He frowned. "You're not going to come?"

"I think I'll just go down this way." She nodded at the cable car.

His frown deepened. "Without kisses? Without even having your hand held?"

Tom giggled. Emily smiled. "I'll manage."

"I don't know if I will," MacPherson grumbled.

"I'm sure you'll do fine," Emily said dryly. "You're very resourceful." She bent down and gave Tom a quick kiss and a stern reminder to behave himself.

"I will," he promised, eyes glowing with excitement at the prospect of their hike.

"You're sure?" MacPherson asked her.

"Positive."

"I——" he hesitated "—didn't scare you off?"

His concern made Emily smile. "No. I just need a little space."

"Well, if you say so." He didn't look convinced.

"You'll take good care of him. I trust you."

Mac's mouth twisted. "Good," he said after a moment. He raked his hand through his hair, then shifted from one foot to the other. "Wait for us at the bottom?"

"Yes." Emily started to turn toward the cable car.

"Emily?"

She looked back over her shoulder at him.

"You can give me your answer then."

"You're leaving for Milan?" MacPherson was furious.

They were walking along the Avenue Michel-Croz,

passing in front of the Alpine Museum, with Tom skipping on ahead as they made their way back toward the apartment after the hike down the mountain. Emily broke the news here, rather than waiting until they were in the apartment. It seemed more sensible, somehow.

MacPherson stopped dead and jerked her to a stop beside him. "What sort of nonsense is that?"

She gave a little laugh and an awkward shrug. "It's not nonsense. It's common sense, really. We're leaving in the morning. We can't impose on you forever, you know."

"I don't know." His voice was a growl.

Emily ignored it. "So while you were hiking down, I just popped over to the station and made reservations. I have friends in Milan and——"

He tugged her around to face him. "So that's your answer?"

She had hoped he wouldn't ask point-blank. She should have known better.

"Yes." It was. The safest one, the only one she thought was right at the moment for herself—and for Tom.

"You really are a coward, aren't you?"

Emily straightened and glared at him. "I am not!"

"No? Then why are you running away? You ran away from Gomez, you run away from me. Getting to be a bit of a habit, wouldn't you say?"

"It's not the same thing at all!"

The look MacPherson gave her was scornful. "Well, perhaps you'll explain the difference."

"Why bother?" Emily pulled away from him and continued walking. "You weren't serious."

She'd decided that before she got all the way down the mountain. No matter how much she might like to dream that tall, handsome strangers would fall in love with her at the drop of a hat, she knew it wasn't true.

It had taken her only a little space to put MacPherson's lips out of her mind and remember Marc's. It had taken only the bump at the bottom of the *téléphérique* to jolt her back to reality—men said things like that all the time. And once they got the woman in question into bed they conveniently forgot all about it.

He was striding alongside her now, one hand on her arm, as if she might disappear if he didn't have a physical hold on her.

"All right," he was saying, "maybe I took it too fast. Maybe I should have strung you along a bit longer——"

"Strung me along!" Emily yelped.

He grimaced. "Bad choice of words. Damn you, Emily. You make me crazy. I can't think when I'm around you. I want—I want——" He didn't say what he wanted. He showed her.

Right there in the middle of the Avenue Michel-Croz, he took her in his arms and kissed her. It was every bit as hungry a kiss as he had given her in the *téléphérique*. It was every bit as demanding, and a bit more desperate. Emily's fingers clutched at his shirtfront. Her toes curled in her shoes. She made *him* crazy?

"The feeling," she muttered against his lips, "is mutual."

"Then why are you leaving?" He had hold of both her arms now. Their faces were scant inches apart. Passers-by were snickering, laughing. Emily barely gave them a thought. She didn't think MacPherson noticed at all. His entire attention was focused on her.

"Because... because you're right," she said at last. "Because I am scared."

"Of me?"

"No. Well, yes. Of you and... and of me." She had to be honest. He wasn't going to let her get away with less. She didn't really want to get away with less.

"Of you?" One dark brow lifted.

"Of what I feel when I'm around you."

He smiled. "You're admitting it, then?"

She ducked her head. "Yes. But I don't understand it! I——

"It's new? Exciting? Tempting?"

"Yes," reluctantly.

His smile broadened. "I feel the same way."

She slanted him a quick glance to see if he was serious. He looked perfectly serious. "We shouldn't," she said firmly.

"Why not? You're not attached? Are you?" he added quickly.

She shook her head.

"And neither am I. So tell me, why shouldn't we?"

"We shouldn't be talking about marriage," she insisted.

"You're not a marrying sort of girl?"

"Of course I am!"

"Well, then..." He lifted his shoulders and spread his palms as if to ask, "What's the problem, then?"

Emily couldn't put it into words.

"Look, Emily, that's what I meant earlier about going too fast. Maybe I did. Maybe I should have kept my peace, played the attentive swain a bit longer before saying how I feel."

They were walking again. Emily picked out Tom far ahead of them now, occasionally glancing back to see what was taking them so long. He'd had a wonderful time hiking with MacPherson. He'd been ecstatic when they'd been reunited with Emily at the base of the mountain. He'd been all set to do it again tomorrow.

Not tomorrow, Emily had told him. But she hadn't told him why. Now she wondered if she'd acted precipitately, panicking about her feelings for MacPherson, rushing off to get reservations so that they could leave for Milan before she had to come to terms with those feelings.

When David had been courting Mari and encountering problems with the attitude of her family, Emily had wondered aloud if Mari was worth the trouble. David had stared at her as if she'd lost her mind.

"It doesn't matter if we go through hell," he'd said, "as long as we come out on the other side married to each other."

"But don't you think, if you don't marry Mari, you might find some other girl?" Emily had protested.

And David had shaken his head, adamant. "I've never felt this way about any other girl. I never will. It'll be Mari or no one, Em. Maybe some day you'll understand."

Emily hadn't for a long, long time. She'd grown to love the woman her brother had married, but she hadn't felt that kind of intense, single-minded attraction herself, even with Marc.

She felt it—or suspected she did—with MacPherson.

And that was the problem.

Might it not be possible that, by leaving tomorrow, she would be throwing away a chance with the one man in the world who would make her happy? Might it not be possible that MacPherson, her heroic stranger, was the one she was destined to love?

"I don't know what to do," she said aloud.

"What do you want to do?"

She shut her eyes and tried to imagine the future, tried to see if somewhere out there she could catch a glimpse of herself and Tom and MacPherson together. Her fingers closed on the key chain, her heart remembered the touch of MacPherson's lips. He wasn't Marc. He hadn't lied to her.

"I want," she said quietly yet clearly, "to give love a chance."

It was every bit the carefree holiday she had dreamed of. And better. Better because while she and Tom walked and fished and swam and played, MacPherson was a part of it.

"Don't let us bother you," Emily said to him almost every day. "You should be writing."

But MacPherson just shook his head. "This is more important," he told her. "This is life, not art."

So they swam together in a pool belonging to an absent friend of his. They hiked in the cool of the mornings along the path that the Arve cut through the mountains. Twice MacPherson took Tom on climbs that brought the boy, sparkly-eyed and exhausted, home to regale Emily with stories of his accomplishments. And Emily listened, grateful and delighted, as she saw him becoming once more the boy he'd been before his mother's death.

It would have happened anyway, she told herself, with time. But that wasn't quite true. MacPherson had a lot to do with it. His interest, his enthusiasm, his patience, his sense of humor, all gave Tom a sense of self-worth and confidence that Emily would have had a hard time helping him develop alone.

This afternoon had been particularly special.

"I need your help," MacPherson had said to them at the breakfast table. "I'm going to do some research, and I'll need your advice."

What this entailed, it turned out, was a mad chase through the streets and over the rooftops of Chamonix.

While MacPherson and Tom pressed themselves against walls and crawled along gutters, then made quick dashes to the next place of cover, Emily's job was to see if she could spot them.

"Utter silliness," she told them, laughing, after she'd tracked them through half the town and finally found them awaiting her at a tiny café, lunch already ordered.

"On the contrary. It's serious business, isn't it, pardner?" MacPherson said to Tom, but he was grinning at Emily.

Tom's own grin nearly split his face. He was breathing hard, and his words came out in gasps. "I'm going to be a writer, too," he reported. "It's fun. Funner than anything." He turned to MacPherson. "How'd you get to be one?"

"Started when I was little. Not much older than you. Seven, as a matter of fact."

Tom's eyes widened. "Really? What'd you do? Crawl through gutters and climb on roofs?"

MacPherson laughed. "No gutters. No roofs. Nothing real at all," he said, dampening Tom's hopes. "I got sent away to school and I hated it. So instead of knuckling down and digging in to make the best of it the way my father told me to, I daydreamed my way out."

As Emily watched, a faraway, wistful look crossed his face. And in it she thought she caught a glimpse of the lonely little boy he must once have been.

"I wrote down my daydreams to save them. They were far more interesting than my real life," he told Tom.

"You didn't get your first book published very early, did you?" Emily asked. "I mean, you weren't 'precocious,' or anything? I don't recall reading that you were," she added hurriedly, feeling a bit foolish.

"Not at all. My first book came out shortly before

my thirtieth birthday. I'm thirty-five now and I've only done three."

"Did you spend all that time writing and not getting published?"

"No. I was never supposed to be a writer."

"What were you supposed to do?" For all that he had found out quite a bit about her, he hadn't been terribly forthcoming about his own background. Emily was glad to find out what she could. The waiter brought the pizza that they'd ordered and MacPherson cut a piece for each of them before he answered.

"I was supposed to be a chip off the old block, go into the family business, work hard, get ahead."

"And did you?"

"After a fashion. I spent some time in Her Majesty's Royal Navy—stalling, I suppose. Trying to put off the inevitable. But I couldn't stall forever, so I finally went to work. Turned out I couldn't work twenty-four hours a day, either. So in my spare time, I wrote. My father wasn't pleased."

"I'll bet he's proud of you now."

"My father's dead," MacPherson said bluntly. "And he never told me he was proud before he died."

Emily put her hand on his. "He should have been," she said softly.

MacPherson's mouth twisted. "That's what I always thought."

"Did he get mad at you when you were a kid, too?" Tom asked. Obviously the thought that MacPherson might have displeased someone astonished him.

"When I wasn't doing what he thought I should be doing. He didn't put up with the daydreaming for long, believe me. A couple of bad reports and I found it hard to sit down." He grimaced at the memory and shifted in his chair. "I don't daydream well standing up, so I had to get to work."

Emily smiled. "But now you write."

"When I have time. I still run the family business."

"Which is what?"

"Oh, electronics mostly. Not exactly my forte, but I have no choice. Since he died, it's my responsibility. My mother doesn't know the first thing about running it. She was never involved. That wasn't her role."

"But surely if you prefer writing, you could get someone else to do it," Emily protested.

"I could. But I won't. I didn't agree with him about a lot of things, but he was right about this—hiring someone to do your work never works as well as doing it yourself. It's a matter of family pride, I guess. But it's also because my mother depends on me." He said it without any regrets, as if he'd long ago come to terms with the demands his family made.

"I don't know if I could do that," she said.

"You already have, haven't you?" Mac's gaze flicked briefly to Tom before coming back to meet hers.

"I'm here because I want to be here, not because of any obligation," Emily said firmly.

"You mean you wouldn't really rather be living it up in Monte Carlo or Paris right now?"

She smiled. "No."

He turned his hand over and folded his fingers around hers. His face was lit with the most tender smile she'd ever seen. "No, Emily Musgrave, I don't suppose you would."

She worried sometimes that Tom would be crushed when the holiday was over and they and MacPherson went their separate ways. But every day it looked less and less as if that might happen.

She began to think MacPherson might really want to marry her after all. And that she might accept if he did. The thing that, more than anything, made her feel this way was that he didn't try to hurry her into making love.

When they weren't racing about Chamonix "doing research," they were reading or laughing or talking or cooking, the three of them together, in MacPherson's apartment. And the conversation focused more on Emily's childhood, on her schooling, on the way she and her brother spent Christmas and summer holidays than on the possibility of MacPherson and Emily sharing a bed.

Of course, the only bed he could offer to share with her was in a room he was currently sharing with Tom!

But her bedroom was her own, and since that first night he hadn't set foot in there, either.

It wasn't because he wasn't interested, either. At least Emily didn't think it was. The looks he gave her, the touches that lingered far longer than they had to, the smiles that made her heart melt, all told her he wanted her badly. But he'd rushed his fences once, and he wasn't doing it again. He was waiting for her to say the word.

It had been seven days since they'd come to Chamonix—seven of the most perfect days of Emily's life. She was glad now that she hadn't panicked and fled to Milan, glad she'd stood her ground, glad she'd taken the risk.

She loved MacPherson. It was time to admit it. For seven days she'd been demure, circumspect, watchful, keeping her own counsel as she got to know him, got to know her feelings for him. And now she knew.

She wasn't sure what event crystallized her thinking. She couldn't pinpoint the moment at which she'd known her heart's desire.

She'd gone to bed last night listening to the gentle clicking of MacPherson's computer, thinking what a comfortable noise it was. She'd awakened once to hear Tom mutter something, and an instant later MacPherson's voice, strong, but gentle, soothing him back to sleep. And when she opened her eyes in the morning and lay in her wide bed alone, she knew that the presence of one man would make it a joy to stay there.

Sandy MacPherson, alias Dominic Piersall. Strong and tough. Thoughtful and tender. Clever and smart. So many sides to just one man, it would take a lifetime to get to know them all. Emily thought she'd like to spend hers doing just that.

Of course, she told herself, as she dressed and brushed out her hair, he might not feel the same way. He might regret he'd ever even suggested it. She wasn't sure how to broach the subject, either.

One could hardly open a conversation by asking, Remember when you suggested the possibility of marrying me?

But there must have been something different about the way she was acting right from the moment MacPherson's bedroom door opened. She was sitting at the table, drinking a cup of coffee and trying to get her thoughts together, and his sudden appearance, though it should hardly have been unexpected, caused her to slop the coffee all over her dress.

"Oh, heavens." She scrambled to her feet, face flaming.

"Are you all right?" He was at her side in a moment.

"F-fine." She was swatting at the spreading brown stains, backing toward the bedroom, intensely aware of him only inches away. "I'm fine," she assured him, needing space, distance, something to aid her sanity.

She didn't get it. He followed her into the bedroom, and his fingers moved to undo the buttons of her dress while her own still fumbled ineffectually.

"You don't have to do that," she mumbled, trying to brush him away, but he shook his head.

"Oh, yes," he said softly. "Oh, yes, I do."

"I don't——" she began. And then, because she couldn't lie, she said, "I do."

And MacPherson smiled, put one finger under her chin and lifted it so that their eyes met, and his were as blue as the ocean and not cold at all.

"That's what I hope you'll say," he whispered. "Will you?"

And Emily knew what he was asking, and knew what her answer would be.

"Oh, yes. I do love you."

It was a moonlit night, and the silvery light spilled down the mountains and through the open windows of Emily's bedroom, bathing the wide bed and Emily, who lay in the middle of it alone.

She wouldn't, though, be alone for long. That much she knew.

All day long she'd felt this need growing inside her, filling her with a hunger and an intensity she'd never experienced before. Every smile, every touch was a portent, a promise. Though they had spent the day as they often did, swimming and hiking with Tom, then Tom and Emily cooking supper while MacPherson typed, the few brief moments they had shared in her bedroom had sealed things between them.

There was anticipation in MacPherson's smile, hunger in his touch. A look of promise as he stroked her arm, kissed her hair. The anticipation had made the promise of the night that much sweeter. And to tell the truth, she'd enjoyed the wait. She'd liked thinking about it while they were hiking with Tom. She'd liked imagining it when they swam and she splashed MacPherson with water and listened to Tom's exuberant laughter when MacPherson caught her and dunked her. It was like heaven, perfect and exhilarating at the same time.

And to know that it would be hers—theirs—forever was almost too much to take in.

Now Tom was tucked up in his bed, she was bathed and dressed in a white nightgown of *broderie anglaise*, and she could hear Mac on the other side of the door, whistling softly as he shut off the shower. She tried to imagine him naked, his dark hair clinging to his skull. She remembered the way he had looked in the pool this afternoon, remembered the hungry glitter in his eyes as he had caught her up in his arms and let her slide down the length of his body, remembered the feel of his arousal, his muttered oath and wry grin, then the way he'd dunked them both. And a good thing, too, Emily thought. She grew hot just recalling it.

The door opened then, and he stood silhouetted in the moonlight. "Emily?"

He looked even taller than usual, his dark hair damp and spiky, his narrow hips clad only in a towel.

"I'm here," she said, and was grateful that her voice didn't quaver.

He came and stood at the foot of the bed, staring down at her, still smiling. But his face was taut, and she saw a hunger that matched her own in the glimmer of his eyes. They traveled the length of her, seeming almost to undress her. Yet at the same time she felt he appreciated the soft cotton that shielded her from his view.

"You're beautiful," he said hoarsely. "So beautiful."

And, for the first time in her life, Emily actually felt that she was. She didn't feel awkward or self-conscious as she often did when she modeled. She didn't feel gangly or giraffelike. She didn't feel as if she was being exploited, as Howell often had said, as merely, "good teeth and bones."

She felt that Mac was seeing her—the whole woman—and was loving her, even without touching her, just as she was.

And then he was beside her, loving her with his hands and his mouth, spreading her hair out against the pillow and sitting back on his heels to admire it in the moonlight, running his fingers through it, then letting them glide down over her shoulders, her collarbone, her breasts.

And Emily, suddenly breathless, found she was shuddering and gasping for air. Her own hands came up and caught his wrists, then slid up his arms, loving the soft feel of the hair as she brushed it the wrong way, loving the silky smoothness of his shoulders and the springy curls on his chest as she trailed her fingers slowly down across it to settle against the knot of the towel.

He shuddered, too, and bit down on his lip. Then he gave a shaky laugh. "You make me wild. I've wanted to do this for days."

"Ditto," Emily whispered, because it was only the truth. All the need she'd been feeling since she'd met him, all the need that had been building inside her for her whole life, the need to be a part of someone, to be known by someone, to share herself fully with someone, seemed to be culminating here and now.

She'd been grasping at it when she'd agreed to marry Marc. She'd been hoping, wishing, desperately, that she could find what David had found with Mari. And she knew now she never had—until tonight.

When MacPherson caught the hem of her nightgown and lifted it with shaking fingers, she helped him, easing her body up to allow him to pull it over her head. When she heard him suck in his breath at the sight of her lying naked in the moonlight before him, she unknotted the towel at his waist and drew a steadying breath, too.

"What'd I tell you?" His voice was ragged. "I want you so much. I need you so much."

And Emily needed him as well. She held out her arms to him, and he came into them willingly, his hands molding her body to his, making her fairly tingle everywhere he touched, making her heart sing so that she threaded her fingers through his hair and curled her toes and slid her foot up the length of his leg.

"God, Emily, what you do to me!" He was kissing her then, and everywhere his lips touched he made his—her cheeks, her shoulders, her breasts, her belly. And Emily twisted beneath him, aching for release, knowing hunger and needing fulfillment.

"Mac!" She reached for him, touched him, and felt him tremble.

"Em, don't. Not yet. You're not——"

"Yes," she said urgently. "Yes, I am. Yes!" And she showed him just how ready she was, drawing him down between her legs, bringing him closer, taking him home.

He bent his head, touched his forehead to hers, kissed her cheek, then her lips. And then he began to move.

It was a rhythm as old as time, as new as the moment, as perfectly synchronized as the two who made it. It seemed to Emily as if it brought a spinning and incoherent world into splendid and perfect focus. She couldn't imagine what she had been worried about. She couldn't imagine ever having doubted.

She could only think that she was glad she had waited until it mattered, until it was right, until the perfect man for her had come along to bring new meaning and purpose and wonder to her life.

"I love you," she whispered against his damp hair. "I love you," she told his smoothly shaven cheek. "I love you," she mouthed against his lips.

And MacPherson rested his head against her breasts, curved one hand around her hip and sighed deeply, settling in, relaxing. "Thank God for that."

It was shortly after noon when the telephone rang.

MacPherson was down in the garden playing catch with Tom. Emily, leaning against the windowsill, watching the men in her life, sighed when the phone rang a second time. Nothing in her wanted to answer it. Nothing in her wanted to break the idyll.

But life was not all holidays. For all that he had claimed they were doing "research," she knew that MacPherson had left his work for quite a few days to be with them. She knew he'd have to work hard to catch up. And it wasn't even his writing, which he loved, it was the family business that demanded his time.

It would no doubt be the family business demanding his time now. What kind of a wife would she be if she begrudged his mother her livelihood?

She picked up the phone.

A cultured British voice said, "Gomez, please."

Emily started, then swallowed. "I—I'm afraid you have the wrong number. There's no one here by that name."

"Is this..." He enunciated a number slowly and carefully.

Emily looked at the phone. "Yes, it is."

"Then I have reached the correct number, madam," the steadfast voice went on. "Would you kindly ask Alejandro Gomez y MacPherson to come to the phone?"

CHAPTER SEVEN

"COME play catch with us," Mac called when she appeared outside the French doors at the bottom of the garden. He was grinning, his dark hair tousled, his bright blue T-shirt clinging damply in the heat. He looked no different from the way he had a minute before when Emily had stood watching him, loving him.

He was different.

He was Alejandro Gomez y MacPherson.

She hadn't believed it at first. She'd stammered his name back at the impatient English gentleman, only to be told what, of course, she already knew.

"Spaniards commonly have both the last names of their parents, madam. Gomez *y* MacPherson. Fetch him quickly, please. It's urgent."

And now Emily had come down the stairs and into the garden as if she were an automaton. She couldn't think, only feel. Her mind was shattered, as if a bomb had just gone off inside her head.

"Come on, Em! Catch!" He tossed her the ball.

She made no move to field it, no move at all except to walk straight toward him. He cocked his head, looking at her now with some concern. His forehead furrowed.

"Emily? What's wrong?"

She was within ten feet now. She stopped and met his gaze. "You have a phone call," she said woodenly, "Mr. Gomez y MacPherson."

Then she turned on her heel and headed back down from where she'd come.

For a moment she heard no movement behind her. Then footsteps, quick and determined on the grass. He caught her arm. "Emily!"

She jerked away, hurrying faster, reaching the stairs. "Leave me alone."

"Damn it, Emily! Let me explain."

"You don't need to explain. It's all quite obvious, thank you very much."

"The hell it is! Listen to me!"

She kept going. She reached the door at last, jerked it open and stepped inside. Grabbing the phone, she thrust it at him. "Your call, Señor Gomez," she fairly spat at him, then stalked back out again.

Tom was still waiting in the garden, looking at her, the joy of the past few days rapidly fading from his face.

"What's the matter, Emmy?" He came up and leaned against her, and she rested a hand on his shoulder, feeling the sun-warmed shirt and the sturdy small body beneath her touch. She lifted her hand and stroked his dark hair.

Why hadn't she seen it? Why hadn't she guessed? She felt the veriest fool. It was there in the hair, in the shape of his face. Emily had always thought Tom had been a compromise between her brother's fairness and Marielena's black hair and eyes. But his coloring was the same as his uncle's, except for the eyes. Even their bone structure was similar. Tom's face was still childishly round, but as he grew older, she felt sure, he would develop his uncle's strong cheekbones, his arched brow and long nose. No wonder Maggie Copeland had thought they were a family!

Her fingers tightened on Tom's shoulder. She was glad at least that she hadn't told Tom yet that she and MacPherson—no, *Gomez*, she corrected herself bitterly—had agreed to marry. They had planned to take him out to dinner tonight and ask him how he felt about the three of them becoming a family.

"I'm not sure we should phrase it as a question," MacPherson had said.

But Emily hadn't worried. "He won't mind. He'll be thrilled," she'd predicted.

And he would have been.

Damn, she thought. Oh, hell and damnation. She felt the anger growing, becoming more than a simmer, roiling up to scald her with its intensity. She would have liked nothing better than to let it all out, but she couldn't—not now, not in front of Tom.

"We're going to have to leave," she said now, keeping her voice carefully calm and controlled.

"Leave? But we just got here!"

"We've been here a week." She was making plans even as she spoke, but before she got any further Mac reappeared.

Emily, with every bone in her wanting to flee, stood her ground.

He looked white-faced and strained.

"We'll be leaving today," Emily said bluntly before he reached them.

He could argue all he wanted, she wasn't giving in. She'd had all of the lies she could take right now. All of Alejandro "Sandy" 'Mac" Gomez y MacPherson. There was nothing he could say that would change her mind.

He shook his head, dazed, and Emily wondered if he'd even heard her. "My mother's had a heart attack," he said.

"You hate my guts."

"Yes."

"You'd like to blind me with a poker."

"Yes."

"You'd like me to sail to the end of the earth and fall off."

"Yes."

"Will you come to England with me?"

"*What*?" Emily, who had been flinging her things out of the drawers and onto the bed, tried to ignore the memories that bed evoked. She spun around and stared at the man who had made those memories with her.

He was standing just inside the doorway, his hands thrust into the pockets of his jeans, his stance battle ready. He'd followed her up the stairs after her perfunctory, "That's too bad." He stood hovering now. She gave him a dismissive snort.

"Will you come to England?" he repeated.

"You're kidding, of course."

"I'm not, dammit!" He jerked a hand out of his pocket and reached toward her but she spun away. "Listen to me, Emily. I have to go to England! I——"

"Go," she said flatly. "I'm certainly not stopping you."

"I know that," he said through gritted teeth. "And God knows I don't want to. Not now at least. But I have to! My mother's very ill. She might...she might not make it."

Emily turned back to face him, drawing a deep breath, praying that she had the tact to say what needed to be said without sounding like the shrew she felt like.

"Look, Alejandro," she drawled his name and had the satisfaction of seeing him wince, "I am very sorry about your mother. Truly I am. She may have been a shrew to Mari, but I don't wish her any ill. But I will be damned if I will go to England with you. I wouldn't go across the street with you! I never want to see you again as long as I live."

"You love me."

She stared at him, furious. How dared he say that?

"You *lied* to me," she reminded him and turned back to jerking clothes out of the wardrobe.

"Would you have given me the time of day if I hadn't?"

"No," she said promptly. "And you knew it, too. Which is why you played your sly, underhanded little game."

She raked a hand through the tangles of her hair. She was hurting terribly. More than she ever remembered hurting in her life. More than when David had been killed. More than when Marielena had died.

Death was, she had heard, a form of betrayal to those left behind. But there had been nothing intentional about David's or Marielena's betrayal. They hadn't meant to hurt her. Alejandro Gomez y MacPherson had.

"Go away. Go to England," she said dully. "Leave me alone. Leave Tom alone."

There was a moment's silence. Then Mac walked across the room and sank down onto the bed. He leaned forward, resting his forearms on his thighs, clasping his hands lightly. His head was bowed. He looked miserable.

Good, Emily thought. He deserved every bit of misery he got. And more. He sat there for what seemed to Emily an unconscionably long time without saying a word. Finally he lifted his head and looked at her.

"I need you to come with me. I know——" he raised a hand to forestall her objections "—that I have no right to ask it. I know you have every right to deny me, but please, Emily...my mother could be dying. Let her see her only grandson."

"I doubt she even wants to see him. She never made a move to before now."

"She couldn't."

"Why?"

"My father——"

"The big bad wolf," she said scornfully.

"He wasn't bad, just...opinionated, determined. A man who thought he knew best and wanted his own way."

Emily just looked at him. "Like father, like son."

MacPherson winced. "Emily, please. Not for me. For her. She wants to see him."

Emily looked away.

"Why on earth do you think I instituted this whole damned pursuit in the first place? My mother wanted to know her grandson!"

"Then she should have written me a letter."

"She didn't think you'd want to hear from her. She was afraid."

Emily stared out the window, saw the *téléphérique* inching its way up the Aiguille du Midi. She wished she were on it.

"She wouldn't beg."

Emily didn't turn. She watched as it passed the crest of the first slope and continued.

"I will," Mac said roughly.

Emily turned then. He was still sitting on the bed, hunched over, his dark hair hanging across his forehead, his eyes hooded, yet clearly pained. She hated him—as much for the love she still felt and which she hadn't conquered yet as for the lies, the subterfuge, and everything else he had done to her. And now this. How could he ask it of her? And yet he was.

"One visit," Mac said hoarsely when she didn't speak. "Just until I get her home from the hospital or..." His voice trailed off, but Emily knew what the "or" meant. It meant the death of Mac's mother. "Just that much, Em."

"For now," she threw at him. "And then what? What other nasty little manipulative trick will you have up your sleeve?"

He gritted his teeth. "It wasn't all nasty and manipulative, dammit. I love you."

She laughed, or tried to. It was a sort of hysterical half laugh, half sob. "Tell me another," she said bitterly.

"Believe me, for God's sake!"

She rolled her eyes. "Believe you? I think you've cried wolf once too often, Alejandro dear." She turned back to the window, her back stiff, her head pounding.

"I love you! I asked you to marry me!"

"Well, I wouldn't marry you if you were the last man on earth!"

"That's not what you said last night."

"You aren't the same man you were last night!"

He shut his eyes. "I am," he said quietly. "I'm the man who loves you."

She whirled on him, furious now. "Spare me all the lies, Alejandro. You don't love me. You wanted what I had, and you figured marrying me was the quickest way to get it."

"No! I——"

"If I could, I would never see you again. Ever!"

He didn't speak then, just sat there, his fists clenching and unclenching against the tops of his thighs. Finally he lifted his head and met her gaze. "Come with me, then——" she opened her mouth, but he forestalled her "—come with me and I swear I'll never bother you again. I'll never ask to see Tom again. I promise."

"Your promises aren't worth much."

"Then I'll put it in writing. You can have your solicitor draw it up. You can take me to court if I violate it. Dammit, Emily. Please."

It was what she'd wanted, after all, to have Tom to herself without fear of threats or arguments, free and clear forever. But she'd never imagined the price it would cost in terms of pain, in terms of loss.

She didn't want to go, though. Still, if she went she would have nothing to reproach herself for—Señora de Gomez would have seen Tom and Emily would be through with Mac. It would be over, complete, *finis*.

She sighed. "All right."

Her dark-haired nemesis met them at Heathrow.

"My cousin and administrative assistant, Pedro Villareal," Mac introduced him with a certain irony. "This is Emily. And Tom."

Pedro Villareal gave Emily a devastating smile, took her hand and raised it to his lips. "I'm pleased to meet you. At last," he said in English every bit as good as Mac's.

Emily muttered something vaguely polite. It was as much as she could manage. She looked from one to the other of them and shook her head. Pedro Villareal looked vastly more like Marielena than Mac did.

Nothing, she thought grimly, was at all what it had seemed.

Mac's mother was hospitalized near her home in Hertfordshire. She had survived the first twenty-four hours with no further attacks, and the doctor's assessment of damage, Pedro told Mac as he drove them northward toward the hospital, was optimistic.

The news seemed to lighten Mac's expression only slightly. His face was still drawn, his eyes troubled. He had been tense and strained from the moment they got the message, though whether from the news about his mother or from the failure of his scheme to get Tom, Emily wasn't sure.

Once his ruse had been discovered, things changed rapidly. They were no longer on foot; a car had miraculously appeared. They hadn't taken the bus back to Geneva; they'd driven. Their seats on the flight from Geneva to Heathrow had been first-class. And they were riding in a plush black Jaguar sedan now.

Tom was goggle-eyed at the turn his life had taken.

Emily was still furious.

Mac was making no attempt to assuage her anger. But at Pedro's assurances he turned slightly in the front seat, looking at Emily out of the corner of his eye. Was he wondering how she'd take the news? Did he expect she would use it as an excuse to leave as quickly as possible? It was tempting, that was certain.

She looked away, pretending not to notice. It was easier to act as if he weren't there—or that she weren't.

She would keep her word. They would visit his mother. They would stay as long as necessary. And then they would be gone.

In the meantime, she would have as little to do with him as she possibly could. To face him, talk to him, pay attention to him all brought the fury and betrayal winging back. She had loved him! *Loved* him! And he, even more than Marc, had been using her!

She couldn't think of it without her throat closing, her eyes blurring, her nails digging into the palms of her hands. Deliberately she locked her fingers together in her lap and stared resolutely out of the window. She tried to listen to Tom's chatter, telling herself she should be glad he was rolling with the punches as well as he seemed to be.

He'd accepted their precipitate flight to England with perfect equanimity. Emily had told him they were going to have to leave, after all. He had no idea that this trip wasn't the one she'd planned.

"We're going to see your grandmother," Mac had told him once it had been settled.

Tom's eyes got very wide. He looked at Emily. "I've got a grandmother?"

Emily spared Mac a hostile glare, then let her expression soften as she knelt down by her nephew. "It's your mommy's mother," she told him. "Mac just got a call that she's in the hospital."

Tom looked stricken. "Is she gonna die, too?"

And Emily felt immediate regret that she'd ever agreed to take Tom to England. It might be fine for his mother—it might devastate Tom. She straightened up, about to object.

"We hope not," Mac said firmly, obviously picking up the same vibrations that Emily was. "But she's had a heart attack, and she needs to be in the hospital for a while until she's better. She'd like you to come and see her."

"She wants to see me?" Tom looked at Emily for confirmation. He remembered, it seemed, some of what his mother had told him about her family.

Mac, too, looked at Emily.

She looked away, giving Tom a tiny nod, all she could manage. "That's what Mac says."

"She would like very, very much to see you, Tom," Mac went on quickly. "Very, very much. Will you come?"

Tom chewed his knuckle, considered it for a moment, then nodded. "Yeah, okay. But I don't want her to die."

"No," Mac said fervently. "None of us does."

And now, Emily thought, it seemed as if they'd get their wish.

Probably, she thought grimly, the older woman was too stubborn to die. Mac wouldn't die if he had unfinished business, Emily was certain of that. She expected his mother to be equally determined and imperious, even laid low as she was now. She was wrong.

Fiona MacPherson de Gomez was far from the regal, patrician woman whom Emily had imagined. She had curly reddish brown hair, only lightly graying, a round face, smiling blue eyes the exact color of her son's—and freckles.

Never in a million years would Emily have expected freckles.

Nor did she expect the welcome. It was ten in the evening when they finally arrived at the hospital.

"Much too late to visit tonight," the ward nurse told Mac, who strode right past her.

Emily, following him, dragging Tom in her wake, simply shrugged at the nurse's consternation. "What Gomez wants, Gomez gets," she muttered, and braced herself to come face-to-face with a female version of the fearsome Alejandro.

Fiona, who was clearly supposed to be lying down and resting, heaved herself up on her elbows to stare as the three of them appeared in the doorway. Her eyes went from her son to Emily to the little boy edging next to Emily's leg. Her expression went from hope to incredulity to unbridled joy. She blinked furiously and in vain. The tears she was so desperate to control slid silently down her cheeks.

Mac moved toward her. "Lie down. Rest. You have to——"

"I have to kiss you, my love," Fiona said and held out her arms to him. "And then I have to welcome my daughter... and my grandson."

Emily opened her mouth to deny it. Mac couldn't have told his mother he'd asked her to marry him. He simply couldn't have! Could he?

She couldn't tell for a moment because Fiona was hugging him close, wiping her eyes, then kissing him again before letting him go and turning to Emily and Tom once more.

Emily looked at Mac and saw at once that he hadn't. But she had no time to figure out a response, for Fiona was beckoning to them.

"Please, dear. Don't be shy. I'm so very glad you came. And——" her voice faltered a moment as her gaze shifted and she took in the little boy who stood so still at Emily's side "—I am especially glad to meet Tom." She smiled at him through her tears.

Emily looked down to see Tom blink back a tear of his own. He took a half a step forward, then hesitated.

Emily knew he was waiting for her. But she couldn't move.

She could do no more than touch his shoulder and say in a low, choked voice, "Can you go say hello to your grandmother, Tom?"

Then, as if the touch and her words released him, Tom did just that. He walked slowly over to the bed and met his grandmother's gaze. "Are you gonna be all right?" he asked her.

She smiled tremulously. "Oh, yes, dear. I certainly am. I certainly am," she repeated, sinking back against the pillows, "now that you're here."

Emily sucked in a fierce breath.

Mac stiffened. "It was a heart attack," he said in a hard, defensive undertone. "A real one. She didn't fake it."

"I didn't imagine she had," Emily replied in a like tone, and looked away from him once again.

Oblivious of the tension behind him, Tom went on. "Did you know my mom?" he asked his grandmother.

"Oh, yes, my love. She was my baby."

"Good. Then sometimes, when I forget, will you tell me about her?"

Fiona reached out and touched his arm and obligingly he moved closer so that her hand came up and brushed his cheek. "I will love doing that, my dear, dear child."

The tears welled up again and she sank back into her pillows once more, obviously spent.

"Mr. Gomez——" the nurse had clearly had enough of touching family reunions at the expense of her patient "—it's very late. Perhaps, tomorrow, with Doctor's approval——"

"Right." Mac, mission accomplished, put his hand on Tom's shoulder and drew the boy back against him. "I think," he said to both the boy and his grandmother, "that the two of you have had enough excitement for one day."

He turned to Tom and said, "How about giving your grandmother a kiss?"

Mac lifted the boy up so that he could drop a feathery kiss on his grandmother's pale cheek.

"Will you come tomorrow?" Fiona asked him. Her gaze went from her son to Emily, pleading in her eyes.

"Tomorrow," Mac promised without even looking at Emily.

"Yeah. See you tomorrow," Tom said brightly. "If you feel better maybe we can go for a walk."

"I don't think she'll be quite ready to walk tomorrow, but maybe soon," Mac told him. "Before long you can push her in a wheelchair. How about that?"

Tom grinned. "Great. If you want me to," he added, looking at the older woman.

"I will look forward to it," she assured him fervently. She reached out once more and caught Emily's hand. "And you, my dear. I thank you so much for your generosity."

"You're welcome," Emily muttered.

She felt like a hypocrite. She felt like pond scum.

And there was no reason for it, she thought angrily as she followed Mac and Pedro out of the hospital. Mac was the one who was to blame, not her.

"She's nice, isn't she?" Tom whispered to her once they were in the back seat of the Jag again, headed toward the Gomez y MacPherson family home.

Emily nodded, not trusting her voice.

"You don't think she's gonna die, do you?"

She shook her head. "I hope not," she managed.

"Me, too." Tom gave a little bounce. "Do you think she really liked me, Em?"

"Of course," Emily said fiercely. "What's not to like?"

"Oh, you know what I mean. I thought maybe she'd be sad, that I'd remind her of Mommy."

Emily put her arm around him and pulled him close. "I'm sure you do, love. But that will make her happy rather than sad, I should think."

Tom sighed and snuggled closer, resting his head against her breasts. "I hope so."

The house was ready for them. The housekeeper, Mrs. Partridge, met them at the door. She hugged Mac, expressing concern about his mother, then relief at what he could tell her.

"Is everything ready here?" he asked her.

She nodded, smiling as he introduced her to Emily. "Tom's aunt," he called her, but her real enthusiasm was saved for "Master Tom."

"We've been looking forward to your coming," she told him, giving the sleepy-eyed boy a smile.

Tom blinked. "You have?"

"Oh, yes."

Emily fixed Mac with an angry look, but he didn't bat an eyelash.

"I think we could all use a light supper before bed," he said to Mrs. Partridge.

"We've beef for sandwiches. Cold ham, tomatoes and salad fixings. I'll be setting it out while you show Miss Emily and Master Tom to their rooms."

Mac smiled. "Thank you, Mrs. Partridge."

The older woman beamed at him. Emily gritted her teeth. She followed him grudgingly as he ushered her up the staircase and into the north wing of the house.

"You'll be right here." He opened a door to a spacious room done in pale blue with a heavy Oriental rug next to a high wide four-poster bed.

"Thank you," Emily said. "Come on, Tom, let's get you in pyjamas."

"This is *your* room," Mac told her. "Tom's down the hall."

"But——"

"We have plenty of rooms, Emily. You don't need to share."

More than that, Emily discovered as she left her own room and followed him, a room had already been prepared for Tom.

And while bile rose in her throat as she thought how easily Mac had expected her to go along with his wishes, how big a fool he expected her to be, she wasn't proof against Tom's joy at the boy-oriented furnishings, the football and the kite which leaned next to the wardrobe.

"Is this... mine?" Tom stopped in the doorway and stared, not daring to hope.

"All yours," Mac assured him.

"Neat." It had sturdy, solid oak furniture, a thick rug near the bed and polished wooden floors that Tom, taking possession, slid sock-footed across with enthusiasm. There was a seat beneath the windows along the far side of the room, and Tom ran directly over and settled in, grinning back at them. "Isn't this neat, Em?"

"Very nice."

Mac scowled at her.

Tom pulled up his knees against his chest and wrapping his arms around them, then leaned to peer out of the tall narrow windows into the darkness. "Do you have a big garden?"

"Yes."

"Is it down there?"

"Yes, and beyond are the stables. Maybe tomorrow we can ride."

Emily gritted her teeth.

Tom looked doubtful, then hopeful. "I've never been on a horse. It was like the hiking, you know. My dad would've taken me, but..."

"Perhaps we can find a pony your size."

Emily had had enough. "I don't think we'll be here all that long." She gave Mac a hard stare.

"I didn't mean buy one," he said mildly. "But several of the people who live hereabouts stable their horses with us. I think we have a few children's ponies that might suit."

"Oh." She felt slightly foolish, forced into being an ogre, always ready to rain on Tom's parade.

And Mac—damn him—knew it. Counted on it. She was sure of that.

"Where's your room?" Tom asked him.

Emily devoutly hoped it was on the other side of the house.

"Next to yours," Mac said. "Right here."

He led them into the room on the other side of Tom's, a wide modern room with teak furnishings, floor-to-ceiling burgundy draperies, and a deep burgundy and navy duvet on the huge bed. In spite of herself Emily remembered last night, remembered the bed they had shared in Chamonix.

Deliberately she turned back into the hall. "Come on, Tom," she said briskly. "You need to get into pyjamas before you have a snack and go to bed."

Tom followed willingly enough, but once he got in his room he moved from the football to the kite, to the set of toy cars he found in one of the bureau drawers. "Look at this, Emmy. Isn't it super? Don'tcha just wish we could live here forever?"

Emily didn't answer. She couldn't if her life had depended on it.

She didn't think she'd sleep all night.

She awoke at ten past ten. Horrified, she bounded out of bed, splashed water on her face, and dressed as quickly as she could. She usually got up before Tom. What would he have got up to in this amount of time? Hastily making her bed, she hurried to Tom's room.

It was empty. His bed was already made. His clothes, which last night had been a jumbled mess protruding from his duffel bag, were now hung on hangers and folded in drawers. His red slippers were tucked neatly under his bed, just as if they'd been there for years. His pyjamas hung in the wardrobe on a peg.

Spinning around, she checked MacPherson's room—she couldn't stop thinking of him that way, even though she tried mentally calling him Alejandro. The door was closed, but she didn't hear any voices within. She certainly wasn't going to look.

Turning, she made her way along the hall and down the stairs, heading for the breakfast room. It faced the back of the house, a cheerful yellow room with a bow window and lots of plants. They had eaten their supper there last night. This morning she found the remains of breakfast waiting for her—eggs, sausage, potatoes, toast, a selection of cereals. MacPherson and Tom were nowhere to be seen.

The door to the kitchen swung open and Mrs. Partridge appeared. "Good morning," she said cheerily. "Up at last, are you? Glad you had such a good sleep. Mr. Alex thought you might not, being you were in a strange bed and all."

"Mr——? Oh," Emily said, figuring out who Mr. Alex must be.

"Should call him Mr. Gomez, now his father's passed on," Mrs. Partridge went on, removing the dirty plates and heading back toward the kitchen. "But he's been Mr. Alex long as I can remember. At school he says they called him Sandy. Or Mac. His father called him Alejandro." Mrs. Partridge didn't give it close to its Spanish pronunciation. "He uses his middle name for his writing. But his mother always called him Alex, and that's good enough for me."

"A man of many identities," Emily said tightly.

"That he is." Mrs. Partridge chuckled, gave Emily one last sunny smile and disappeared into the kitchen.

Seconds later she was back. "He wasn't quite sure what you'd like to eat, so I fixed up a bit of everything."

"Toast," Emily said. "Just toast."

Mrs. Partridge made a tsking sound. "You're bones, child. Skin and bones. Model, he said you were. Well, not any more. You eat around here." She picked up a plate and piled it high with eggs, sausage and potatoes. She frowned a moment, then added a piece of toast on the top.

A peace offering? Emily wondered as the older woman thrust it at her. "Here now, lovey, sit yourself down and try this."

"Really, I don't—I need—— Where's Tom?"

Mrs. Partridge nudged her into a chair. "Don't you worry about the boy. Mr. Alex will take good care of him. They've gone riding." She glanced at the clock on the dresser. "Shouldn't be gone too much longer."

"Riding? But Tom hasn't——"

"Got him a little pony. Belongs to Veronica's girl, but Lucy's grown out of him. Topper, he's called, and your Tom was that thrilled. They make a pair." Mrs. Partridge beamed.

Emily had no idea who Veronica was. Or Lucy. She didn't care. She felt as if her life were slipping completely out of control. She was simply grateful that Mrs. Partridge had referred to him as "your Tom." She was beginning to wonder if anyone remembered that he was.

She was going to have to start making sure that they did. Otherwise, that devious Gomez y MacPherson would have Tom away from her before she could turn around.

"I want to see him as soon as he comes back," she said firmly. "He shouldn't have gone riding without telling me."

"Well, now, he isn't going to get hurt. Mr. Alex will watch him like a hawk."

The predator image was more accurate than Emily would have liked. She took a bite of toast and chewed vigorously. Mr. Alex was going to hear a word or two about his presumptions when he came in.

It was unfortunate, then, that twenty minutes later, when he did, Tom was as bright-eyed and rosy-cheeked as Emily had ever seen him.

"I rode 'im, Em! I rode Topper!" He virtually flew across the room and bounced up and down in front of her. "You shoulda seen me!"

"I would have," Emily said, "if anyone had bothered to tell me you were going."

Tom's grin faded. "You were sleepin' an' Mac said you needed your rest, you'd been working real hard an'..." He looked at Mac to see if he was conveying the sense of what his uncle had said.

"We didn't want to disturb you," Mac said smoothly.

"I wouldn't have minded," Emily said. "I would have preferred it," she added pointedly.

"Are you mad, Em?" Tom asked worriedly.

"Not at you."

Tom's worried look moved from her to Mac, and Emily cursed herself for upsetting him. It wasn't Tom's fault! She gave him a hug. "Don't worry, lovey. I'm glad you had a good time."

He brightened at once. "I did. It was super. Next time you can come. Emmy can ride with us next time, can't she, Mac?"

Emily glanced up to find Mac's blue eyes on her. "Oh, yes," he said.

"I don't ride," Emily told him.

"You can learn."

"We won't be here long enough." She met Mac's gaze with a defiant one of her own.

He didn't reply at once, just looked at her. It was disconcerting what those blue eyes could do to her still. They could make her weak with longing, aching with remembrance. It took everything she had in her to focus on the lies Mac had told her, the lies on which their relationship had been based, but she managed. She kept her expression stony cold.

"I'd like to take Tom to see my mother this afternoon," he said at last. "Is that all right with you?" His tone was exaggeratedly polite. Mrs. Partridge simply stared.

"Fine," Emily said, her voice clipped. "One o'clock?"

"That would be good."

"I'll have him ready."

Mac nodded. "Thank you." He turned on his heel and went out, shutting the door quietly behind him.

CHAPTER EIGHT

"WE WON'T be here that long," Emily had told Mac.

She said the same thing over and over to herself, walking in the woods, sitting in the parlor, looking out of the window over the garden. "We won't be here long enough for Tom to get attached."

She hadn't known it would take a matter of hours, at most a day, for that to happen. She hadn't counted on the welcoming home, the room of his own, the pony called Topper, the boy down the lane who was just his age, not to mention Grandma Fiona and Uncle Mac.

Emily wasn't sure exactly when Tom had made the connection about Mac.

She certainly didn't tell him. And when she confronted Mac about it the following night, he had claimed he hadn't either. Emily supposed it must have been Fiona. It didn't matter. By bedtime the second night, Tom knew.

"How come Mac didn't tell me he was my uncle?" he said when she was tucking him up in bed and kissing him good-night. "You said he was your friend. How come you didn't tell me? Was it 'cause my mother had a fight with them?"

Unwilling to lie, Emily nodded. "More or less."

Tom sighed. "I thought so. Grandma says she's really sorry about that. She says they were wrong."

"Good," Emily said, though she didn't feel very good about it at all. She supposed she should be glad that Fiona regretted what had happened, but it seemed too little and far too late, at least as far as Mari and David were concerned.

But, "It is, isn't it?" Tom said, and he was smiling again.

He'd been smiling most of the day, and for that at least Emily had to be pleased. She held his hand in hers and felt his fingers curve around her own.

"I'm glad we can be friends now," Tom went on. "If I can't have a dad, I'm glad at least that Mac's my uncle. We're goin' riding again tomorrow, Emily. Eric's coming. You know, the boy I met today, the one who lives down the way. Can you come too?"

"I don't know." Emily didn't want to encourage the riding. She didn't want to encourage the friendship with Eric. She wanted Fiona to get well, and she wanted to be gone.

"We aren't really leavin' soon, are we?" Tom looked worried now, and that was exactly what Emily was afraid of.

"I . . . don't know. We can't impose," she said stiffly.

"We're not imposing. This is a big house," Tom told her. "Too big, Grandma says. She says it needs kids in it." He looked hopeful and wistful at the same time.

Emily gritted her teeth. Unfair, Fiona, she thought.

"Maybe some day it will have," she said briskly. "Now, then, it's time for you to go to sleep."

"Other kids?" Tom sounded sad. "Will they have my room, do you think?"

"What? Oh, I don't know. It won't matter. It's not really your room, Tom. It's——"

"It is!" His chin lifted. His brown eyes challenged her. "It is my room. Uncle Mac said it is."

Uncle Mac. Damn Uncle Mac, Emily thought.

"I'm not going to argue with you about it, Tom." She bent and dropped a kiss on his forehead. "Now, you've had a big day and you're tired, so let's stop talking and you can go to sleep."

"It is my room," Tom muttered as Emily moved toward the door.

Emily pretended not to hear. She shut off the light. "Good night, Tommy." She tried to make her voice sound light. She didn't think she was much of a success.

"G'night," Tom whispered. And when she was almost out of the door, he added, "Please come ridin' tomorrow, Emmy. Please."

She paused. "We'll see."

She went riding with them in the morning. Not because she wanted to ride, not because she had any burning desire to be with Mac, but because she felt she had to protect her interest. If she didn't, she could see Tom slipping away.

They rode across from the stables across a meadow toward a small stream-fed lake that Tom informed her was a great place for fishing. "Uncle Mac says maybe we can fish there this afternoon," he told her, his eyes bright with excitement.

"I thought you were going to see your grandmother this afternoon," Emily said. She didn't bother glaring at MacPherson, who was riding a large sorrel gelding alongside her.

"After we go see his grandmother," MacPherson said.

Emily did glare at him then. "Don't you have any work to do?"

"It gets done," he said easily. "I have my priorities."

And right now his priority seemed to be spending every waking moment with Tom. Emily knew she shouldn't be surprised after witnessing the lengths to which he'd been willing to go to get the boy. Still, she found it irritating.

"Are we gonna stop and get Eric?" Tom asked his uncle after they'd skirted the pond and were headed into the shady woods.

"If you like."

Tom nodded. "It's more fun with him. He's a good rider, Emily. Wait'll you see."

Emily hadn't met Tom's new friend Eric Barnes yesterday. She'd heard about him over tea, and over a game of Fish in the evening, and at bedtime. She had mixed feelings about the acquaintance. It wasn't that she didn't want Tom making friends; it was just that she knew they were leaving soon. What good would it do if Tom made friends and lost them again?

But she couldn't explain that to Tom. And she was sure Mac wouldn't. He might have said he wouldn't fight her for Tom, but there was no reason she could see for believing him. Besides, it was all too clear that he wouldn't need to. Tom would likely do it for him.

She steeled herself to meet Eric.

He was a cheerful little boy, towheaded, with a tooth missing in front and scabs on both knees. Exactly the sort of friend she would like Tom to have. Back in the States. Not here.

Emily even liked his mother—a brisk, no-nonsense woman named Anne, who was weeding her garden with two toddlers underfoot, and was delighted when Mac offered to take Eric with them for a while.

"You're sure? He can be a handful," she said candidly.

"I'm sure," Mac said. "We've a handful of our own." His gaze went to Tom; and Anne smiled, first at him, then at Emily.

"I'm so glad you've come," she said to Emily. "There aren't any boys Eric's age nearby. Or there haven't been until now."

Emily opened her mouth to explain that she and Tom wouldn't be staying, but Mac cut in, "We won't be more than an hour. See you later, Anne." And he was herding Emily and the boys off down the lane without allowing Emily another word.

Scowling, recognizing what he was up to, Emily rode on. She wasn't pleased.

He tried to make conversation several times during that hour. She barely replied, pretending interest in the scenery or preoccupation with her horse. She didn't want to talk to Mac, didn't want to think about him. It was still too hard, the betrayal too new. She would deal with him now because she had to, for Fiona's sake. But she wished she never had to see him again as long as she lived.

When they got back to the stables before lunch, she turned her horse over to Barnaby, the groom, as quickly as she could. Eric's mother had invited Tom to stay for lunch, promising to bring him back before he had to go with Mac to visit Fiona. If Emily had thought riding with Mac in the company of two six-year-olds was difficult, it was nothing compared to riding with him without any children at all.

She had lagged behind, then cantered ahead, anything to avoid conversation with him. It was too painful. Now she hoped she could escape to the house without having to say anything else.

Her luck didn't hold.

Mac caught her arm just as she was closing the stable door. "This isn't like you, Emily."

She scowled at him. "How do you know what's like me? You scarcely know me."

He shook his head. "I think I know you better than anyone. I know how much you care, how much you want Tom to be happy."

"And so you'll use it against me. Thank you very much," she said bitterly.

"Dammit, Emily, I'm not trying to use it against you. I want the best for you, too!"

"Of course you do." There was no way he could mistake the sarcasm in her voice. She managed to jerk away from him and stalked on toward the house.

He caught up with her. "You remember the old expression, 'biting off your nose to spite your face'?"

"I suppose you think that's what I'm doing." She hurried on, not looking at him.

"I think you could make a good case for it."

"I'm supposed to be grateful you lied to me? I'm supposed to welcome this manipulation with open arms?"

"I didn't lie!"

Emily snorted. "By omission you certainly did. And don't try to salve your conscience with hair-splitting definitions. Or maybe you don't even have a conscience." She felt a brief twinge of satisfaction at the heightened color along his cheekbones.

He started to reply as they were coming up the steps, but Pedro opened the door. "Telephone," he said to Mac. "It's Marzetti, from New York. The call you've been waiting for."

Mac ground his teeth. "We haven't finished discussing this, Emily," he said.

"You might not have," Emily countered and brushed past him into the house, grateful to Mr. Marzetti, whoever he was. She didn't want to hear anything more from Alejandro Gomez y MacPherson, especially not anything about how she really ought to feel.

He knew damn all about feelings. Mari had certainly been right about that!

* * *

She was reading in her bedroom when Mac was supposed to go and pick Tom up and take him to visit Fiona that afternoon. She had asked Mrs. Partridge for a tray in her room at lunch, deliberately shutting herself off from the rest of the household. She had felt faintly guilty about making more trouble for the housekeeper, then told herself angrily that Mac was right, she was always far more concerned about everyone else than about herself.

The knock on the door, shortly before two, startled her, making her afraid that Mac had come to renew battle. Then, realizing that it was part of Mrs. Partridge's duties to pick up her lunch dishes, she relaxed again.

She was surprised when it was neither of them. Pedro stood there, looking as if he would rather be somewhere else.

"Sorry to disturb you," he apologized at once. "I was afraid, when you didn't come to lunch, you might not be feeling well."

"I'm fine," Emily said. "I just didn't want——" She stopped, embarrassed, not really wanting to drag Pedro into her squabble with his cousin. But Pedro seemed to know what she was going to say.

"Mac said you didn't come because you didn't want to see him," he said frankly. "He said you'd be pleased to hear he's gone to New York."

"Gone——?"

"The phone call. We have been having some problems in the New York office. They could have been resolved if he'd been around, but..." Pedro stopped, obviously aware that he was treading on dangerous ground.

"He should have stayed around," Emily said sharply. "Everyone's life would have been better if he'd just tended to business."

"Maybe," Pedro said, "but I think Tía Fiona might..." He didn't have to finish his sentence. Emily knew he thought his aunt wouldn't have survived long without the incentive of seeing her grandson. She thought he might be right, though she wasn't admitting it.

"Good," she said briskly. "I'm glad he's gone."

Pedro's thin lips managed a smile. "Yes, but he wanted me to ask you to pick Tom up this afternoon and take him to see Tía Fiona."

"Me?" Emily stared at him.

Pedro gave a helpless shrug. "It is what he asked."

"I don't want——"

"I can do it. He thought you would rather..."

"Always thinking, that's our Mac," Emily said bitterly. Of course, given the choice, she would prefer taking Tom to the hospital. She would want to be there, rather than simply send him with Pedro. Tom still didn't know Pedro well. Neither, for that matter, did Emily. "We couldn't just...skip a day?"

Pedro shook his head. "We would rather you did not. The doctors are pleased with Tía Fiona's progress. We would not want to delay it in any way, would we?"

"No, of course not," Emily said, and, even though she resented it, it was quite true.

"Just let me clean up a bit."

"I called Mrs. Barnes. She'll be expecting us in half an hour."

Us. Naturally, Emily thought, Mac wouldn't trust her to go on her own. Naturally he'd send Pedro along with her. And, even if she put the most charitable construction on it possible, that he knew she wasn't comfortable driving on the left, that he knew she didn't really know her way to the hospital yet, she still felt that familiar flare of anger at his high-handed tactics.

"I'll be ready," she said sullenly.

Before she could get out of the door, Mrs. Partridge called her to the phone.

"For me?" Emily frowned.

"It's Mr. Alex."

Emily grimaced. "What?" she said into the receiver.

"You're going to the hospital with Tom?"

She was surprised it was a question. "Just as you decreed, my lord."

She heard an angry whoosh of breath. "Say what you like to me, Emily. Just don't take it out on my mother."

"What do you think I am?"

"I'm not sure any more," he said roughly. "But she's still weak. She needs all the hope we can give her. And Tom is that hope. Don't tell her you're taking him away."

"We agreed——"

"We agreed that I wouldn't stop you after she was home and well. She doesn't know anything about that agreement, and I won't have you telling her."

"You're going to lie to her, too?"

"Dammit, Emily! I don't want her to die!"

Emily was immediately contrite. "I know that," she said quietly.

"So, please——" it sounded as if he had trouble with the word "—don't say anything to her." A pause. "Emily?"

"I won't," Emily said in a low voice. "But you're going to have to tell her some time. I'm not going to have her think this is my fault."

"I'll tell her," he said heavily. "In good time."

"Soon."

"In good time," he repeated. "Don't rush things."

"I want to get on with my life."

"You could have a perfectly good life where you are now."

"No."

"Yes, dammit, Emily. If you'd stop being so stubborn——"

"Me? Stubborn? Go look in a mirror, Señor Gomez! There's stubborn!"

"Oh, for heaven's sake, Emily. You know I had to do it. You know you wouldn't have let me near you otherwise."

"And a good thing it would have been, too!"

He bit out an expletive. "We're going to have to get this straightened out. But right now I have to go to New York."

"Good riddance," Emily muttered and hung up before he could say another word.

Pedro waited in the car while she went in to collect Tom at the Barneses'. He was bright-eyed and eager to show her Eric's house and only briefly disappointed that Mac wasn't there. Emily chivvied him along as quickly as she could without being rude to Eric or his mother.

In fact she would have liked to stay and chat with Anne Barnes. She was a cheerful, take-life-as-it-comes sort of woman, whose approach to child-rearing appealed to Emily. It would have been nice to get to know her better, to have her as a friend.

But Emily didn't dare. She wouldn't be here long enough. It would be bad enough taking Tom away, assuaging his miseries at leaving. It would be even harder if she had trouble tearing herself away, too.

So she forced herself to remain distant, declining when Anne invited her and Tom for lunch the following afternoon, regretting the other woman's disappointment when she said no.

"I understand, though," Anne Barnes said, walking them to the door. "You've got a life of your own. I guess I thought for a moment you might be like me, cooped up in some Victorian spaceship that hurtles through space with only me and the kiddies aboard—until Douglas gets home for tea, anyway." She grinned and Emily felt even worse.

"Maybe some other time," she said. "I would like to, it's just——"

"Don't worry about it. We'll have a chance," Anne said. "I hope."

"I coulda gone," Tom told her on the way to the car. "I'm not gonna be busy tomorrow. Am I?"

"I—probably." Emily didn't want to discuss it. She helped Tom with his seat belt, then got in the car next to Pedro. Nothing more was said on the way to the hospital.

Fiona was sitting up in her bed, waiting for them. She looked anxious when they came around the corner, but the moment she spied Tom her eyes lit up and a smile wreathed her face. Emily thought it might fade a little when she saw who was accompanying him. But Mac's mother's smile widened even further when she saw Emily.

"Come in, come in, my dear." She gave Tom a hug, then held out her arms to Emily.

Slowly, reluctantly, Emily went into them. It was a bittersweet moment. Fiona was a kind woman, a loving woman, a woman Emily could have related to well in another time, other circumstances. Missing the warmth of her own mother's love, she would happily have basked in Fiona's.

But she was going to leave. She was going to take Tom and hurt his grandmother. And, knowing that, she couldn't relax in the older woman's embrace.

Fiona noticed. She dropped her arms and gave Emily a sad smile. "You're remembering the past, aren't you? Remembering Mari and . . . and David?" It was hard for her to say Emily's brother's name, hard to acknowledge the painful schism that had existed between them.

Emily nodded. Of course she was remembering that. But even more she was remembering new, more painful breaks.

"It was foolish," Fiona said. "Very, very foolish. My husband was a strong man, a powerful man, a man who loved very deeply, but also a man who couldn't understand people were not always going to want to do what he wanted them to." She smiled again, this time wistfully. Then she turned her attention to Tom. "How would you like to go out on the grounds today? They've brought me a wheelchair."

Tom nodded. "Can I push it?"

"I certainly hope so," his grandmother said. She asked Emily's help in getting into the chair. "I hate being so weak," she grumbled. "I used to walk every day, four miles. Now I can't walk four yards."

Emily felt Fiona's weakness as she eased the older woman into the chair. "Are you sure you should be doing this? It's only been a few days."

"The sooner the better." Fiona gave her a determined smile. "I want to get home. I want to see my grandson there, not in some musty old hospital."

So Emily helped her, feeling like a heel because she should say something, should tell Fiona that she was leaving as soon as possible, taking Tom with her, going as far away as she possibly could.

"Take it easy now," one of the nurses cautioned Tom as he steered his grandmother toward the door. "You go slowly."

"I will." And Emily could see he meant it. His little face was set with determination, his tongue tucked in the corner of his mouth as he concentrated on maneuvering the chair through the door she held open for him.

Once outside, as Fiona had doubtless realized, Tom found plenty to interest him. He would push the chair a few yards, then point out something in the gardens through which they walked, and Fiona would urge him to take a closer look. It meant that he expended plenty of energy dashing here and there, coming back to give his grandmother breathless reports on what he discovered; it also meant that Fiona had a chance to talk to Emily.

"I wanted Mac to find you," she said quite candidly. "I knew you shouldn't have to bear all the responsibility for Tom."

"I wanted to!" Emily said before she could stop herself.

Fiona nodded and patted her hand. "Of course you did, my dear. But you have a life, too. You're young. It's such a burden."

"I never saw it that way."

"No." Fiona smiled up at her. "I don't suppose you did. You're a very caring person. I can see that. And you obviously love Tom a great deal. I'm so glad you've decided to share him with us."

Emily bit her tongue, hating Mac for not letting her tell his mother the truth.

"It's good for Tom to be here. Good for all of us. Tell me about Mari and your brother."

Emily looked down at her, startled at the request. From what Mari had said, the family had never wanted to know. She said as much now, unable to keep all the bitterness from her voice.

Fiona sighed. "We cared. We always cared. Alfredo wasn't used to being disobeyed, that's all. I tried to talk to her, to tell her to give him a chance."

"You did?" It was the first Emily had heard of it.

"Oh, yes. Alfredo wouldn't contact them. He was a stubborn man. But Mari was just as stubborn."

"It seems to be a family trait," Emily muttered under her breath.

"What?" Then Fiona laughed and shook her head. "Oh, my, no. Just Mari and Alfredo. Not Alex. Alex was the peacemaker. Or he tried to be."

Emily stared at the older woman, not quite sure she could believe her ears.

"He was always caught in the middle. He was such a quiet boy. Willing. Alfredo never understood him. He only understood the spitfires—like Mari."

Mari could be a bit of a spitfire, Emily would grant that. But she could scarcely credit the notion that Alejandro Gomez y MacPherson was the quiet, willing, peacemaking sort. Her doubts must have showed on her face, for his mother went on,

"You know he was sent to get Mari to see sense when she wanted to marry your brother? Well, he didn't really want to. It was duty to his father that sent him. He feels very strongly about duty and responsibility, our Alex. He was always trying to please his father. He didn't want to fail about something as important as this. I could have told him that Mari was too much like her father. He would have no choice."

Fiona watched Tom as he raced over toward the bed of roses. "Tom is nowhere near as willful as his mother. He must take after his father?"

"Yes," Emily said. "There's a lot of David in him."

"Good. Mari was too much like her father for her own good. Neither of them would give an inch. And everyone suffered for it." Fiona reached out and grasped one of Emily's hands in her own. "There has been enough suffering," she said. "We must go on from here, all of us, and give Tom the best life possible.'' Her eyes lifted and sought Emily's. ''You agree?''

Emily's eyes closed for a moment, then opened and met Fiona's briefly before flickering guiltily away. ''Yes,'' she murmured. ''Oh, yes.''

CHAPTER NINE

IT WAS impossible to dislike Fiona de Gomez. It was impossible to enjoy the idea of, before long, taking Tom away from her for good. But it was equally difficult for Emily to contemplate staying, though Fiona seemed to take it for granted that she would. As far as Mac's mother was concerned, when she came home they would all be one big happy family.

When Emily left that afternoon, Fiona clutched her hand. "I'll see you tomorrow, won't I?"

Emily, knowing all the while that it was a bad idea, saw the eagerness in Fiona's eyes and could only hide her reluctance and say yes.

And so Fiona saw her the next day. And the next.

Over the coming week, since Mac didn't come back, their visits continued daily, and, despite Emily's better judgment, a relationship began to blossom.

Fiona grew stronger every day, going a bit farther in the wheelchair, taking more and longer slow walks along the sunlit corridors of the hospital.

"I'm getting my strength back," she told Emily cheerfully, "so I can keep up with that young scamp." Her fond gaze went to Tom who was skipping on ahead of them. And the love in her eyes and the pain she knew Fiona would feel when they left made Emily feel mere inches tall.

But, almost worse than her interest in Tom, Fiona's concern about Emily made her feel even smaller.

She delighted in Emily's company, too, asking questions, then reveling in the stories Emily told her about her growing-up years in the Midwest, about the trials and tribulations of her years modeling. She was genuinely interested, genuinely caring, and certainly regretful that she hadn't had the chance to do the same with Emily's brother David.

"It was a mistake," she would say sadly from time to time. "But what could I do? What *could* I do?"

But then she would smile gamely and forge on, telling Emily stories in turn—stories about Mari and, worse, stories about Mac.

It hurt to listen, to hear his mother's view of what a wonderful son Mac had always been, of what a kind and thoughtful man he'd become. It made Emily's heart twist when story after story supported Fiona's claim that Mac had always put the family's good above his own, had always tried to do the best for his father, for Mari, and for her.

"He always cared," she said. "From the time he was little, he was the one who tried to make things right for everyone."

She seemed to take it for granted that, of course, he'd done the same for Emily and Tom.

Fiona had no idea how the land really lay between Emily and her son. She had no idea of the subterfuge he had used to get Tom here. She thought he was every bit as wonderful as Emily once had thought him. But she was his mother. What else could she think?

Nothing that Emily could tell her. So she hugged her pain to her heart and didn't enlighten Fiona.

Days went by, a week, then two, and Mac didn't return.

Emily had mixed feelings about his continued absence. It was good because it meant she didn't have to see him. It was bad because she found she needed his continual presence to feed her anger. It was too easy, sitting there listening to Fiona every day, to forget his lies and manipulations. It was much too simple just to let herself believe that everything really was going to work out as well as Fiona believed it would.

But she didn't realize how complacent she'd become until Fiona looked at her speculatively one afternoon and said, "You and Alex would make a good pair."

Emily started and stared at the older woman. "No!" she burst out before she could stop herself.

Fiona sighed. "Ah, there's someone else, is there?"

"N-not really," Emily conceded, not wanting to lie any more than she had to. "I just...just don't agree. We're totally different."

"You both love Tom."

"Yes, but——"

"And you both want what's best for him."

"I know. But——"

"So what could be better?" Fiona spread her hands as if they were holding the happy solution to all their problems.

Emily shook her head. "It isn't that simple."

"Isn't it?" Fiona asked her.

"I don't think so," she said, more gently than she felt.

It was, doubtless, the solution that Mac had worked out himself. Everything Fiona had said about him only confirmed it.

Glutton for family duty and responsibility that he was, Mac must have decided at some point, shortly after meeting her, that taking Tom away from his aunt wouldn't be the best idea. A boy would need a mother, a woman who loved him, cared about him. And to get that woman, pragmatic, dutiful Mac had asked her to marry him.

If only he hadn't said he loved her!

All the other lies Emily could understand. Not that one.

Who would possibly believe that he, world-famous author, talented and forceful CEO of a multinational corporation, could have fallen in love with a nobody like her?

Of course she'd been a face on billboards, a smile in magazines. But that wasn't really her. And what was there of her that might otherwise appeal? She'd had only a year of college, no real career to fall back on now that her modeling was over, nothing to recommend her beyond her pretty face.

Surely Mac was smart enough to know that. Other men might fall for the cardboard woman. He never would.

He must really think she was stupid and naive to believe he had.

Marc had certainly thought so, she remembered bitterly. And maybe they were right. She'd been fooled completely, not once, but twice.

She pressed her lips together and fought against the thickening feeling in her throat. "I'd better be getting on," she told Fiona. "Come along, Tom," she said to the boy, who was playing with toy cars on the floor. "Say goodbye to Grandma now."

"And I'll see you tomorrow," Fiona promised.

Tom scooped up his cars and went to give his grandmother a kiss on the cheek. "When are you coming home?"

"Not long now," Fiona said, her voice brightening as it always did when she contemplated the possibility. "Next week, the doctor thinks." She beamed at Emily. "I can hardly wait."

Emily smiled faintly, feeling smaller than ever, and made her escape.

* * *

She shouldn't even wait, she told herself when she got home. She wasn't doing Fiona any favors by prolonging the agony. She ought to take Tom now and vanish. It wasn't keeping to the letter of what she had promised Mac. But he could hardly complain. Not after what he'd done to her.

She needed to do something, though. She still wasn't over him and she knew it. She still dreamed about him at night. She still thought about him by day. It was worse, she was sure, because she was living in his house, seeing the family portraits, hearing the family stories, settling into the family routine.

And there was no doubt she was settling in—as was Tom. If she waited much longer, it would be impossible to wrench him away.

If Mac were back, she would tell him so. She wouldn't care if he agreed or not. But he didn't come.

And every time she asked Pedro when he might return—which wasn't often because she didn't want to be thought interested—she got only a vague shrug of the shoulders and a helpless shake of the head.

"He will come as soon as he is able," was all Pedro said.

Well, Emily wasn't waiting. Didn't dare. She would have to figure out a way to leave without telling him, then. She certainly had no intention of confiding in Pedro. He would do everything in his power to make sure she was right here until Mac's return.

She waited, then, until he had taken Tom riding that afternoon. Then she slipped into Mac's library and called for a train schedule.

It was perhaps three miles to St. Alban's. Surely she could manage to get a taxi to come and take her and Tom to the station? She would just have to do it when Pedro was otherwise occupied.

He was, she now understood, Mac's right-hand man, the one who kept things going in the family business while Mac wrote, the one who kept things on an even keel while Mac coped with vanishing nephews and intractable guardian aunts, the one who was expected to keep her in line until he could get back and take over again.

Yes, she would have to be wary of Pedro, she thought as she thanked the stationmaster and hung up the phone.

"Going somewhere, are you?"

She spun around to see Mac lounging against the doorframe.

Her heart leapt at the sight of him. All her anger, all her hatred, all her resolutions were nothing in the face of the emotions he excited by his very presence—emotions not like anger and hatred at all. She clenched her fists, trembling, trying desperately to stop.

"Yes," she said, and was grateful that her voice barely quavered. "I'm going home."

One dark brow lifted. "Home?" He made it sound as if she didn't have one.

She nodded stiffly. "To the States. Your mother is much better. She'll be coming home soon. Next week, the doctor said. I want to leave."

His jaw tightened. "You said you'd stay till she came."

"But it's been weeks! It's pointless to stay any longer!"

"Not for Tom," he said quietly.

"That's not fair."

"Life's not fair, Emily."

No, it wasn't. If it were fair she could hate him now, she could turn her back on him, cut him dead. She blinked rapidly, then swallowed against the tightening in her throat.

"Has it been that bad here?" he asked her gently.

"Of course it hasn't been bad."

"You got along all right with my mother?"

"Yes."

"And Pedro?"

"Of course."

"Then why can't you stay?"

"You know why!"

"Because of us."

She wanted to yell at him, to scream that there was no "us'. But she didn't trust her voice. Mutely she shook her head, then turned away, trying to ignore him, hoping he would take a hint, go away.

Instead she heard his footsteps, felt his approach.

"Good," he said softly.

Her gaze swung sharply to meet his. "What's good about it?"

"You still care. In spite of yourself."

And without giving her even a second to deny it, he closed the remaining distance between them, put his arms around her and touched his lips to hers.

It was as if he'd set her on fire. In spite of everything she knew, everything she didn't want to happen, she had no control over her feelings at all once his lips touched hers. It didn't matter if he'd lied or not, if he loved her or not. This was the man, unfortunately, to whom she'd given her heart.

Could they make a marriage of it despite their beginning? Emily wondered. Could such a marriage survive? Was love on one side and duty on the other enough to build on?

Emily remembered David telling her she'd know, perhaps even in spite of herself, when she met the man who belonged to her. She remembered his saying that the road might not always be smooth. "But you have to take it, Em," he'd told her. "You have to try."

Mac's lips were moving, hard and warm and persuasively over hers, asking for a response. And, helpless to resist, Emily gave it to him.

His arms tightened, holding her close, sheltering her, and when his lips finally lifted infinitesimally from her own he sighed and rested his forehead against hers.

Shaken to the core, Emily couldn't say a word. It was useless, she thought. She had no defense.

And when he said, "Stay?" she shivered and took the leap, nodding her head against his shoulder, sighing, "Yes."

He smiled at her over the breakfast table the next morning. He, not Pedro, came with them on their morning ride. He drove them over to the hospital to see his mother shortly before noon.

Fiona was delighted, of course, and the look she gave Emily when she saw Mac hovering over her spoke of her pleasure that, despite Emily's objection that they had little in common, they seemed to be getting along.

She didn't say anything, however, didn't ask any questions, just waited. But the tears were quite real when, as they were leaving, Mac bent down to kiss her and said, "Hurry up and get out of here. You've got a wedding to attend."

Her eyes went to Emily then, damp and hopeful as they scrutinized her pale face. And Emily, for her part, could only manage to nod and cross her fingers.

"Oh, my dears," Fiona said, clutching Mac's hand tightly and reaching for Emily's. "I am so pleased."

"So am I, Mother," Mac said.

Emily hoped it was true. It was so fragile, this peace between them. And it owed more to emotion than good sense. But David and Mari had married for love, not reason. Their marriage, however brief, had been good.

Emily hoped for the best.

Pedro was waiting on the doorstep when they returned. "All hell has broken loose in New York again," he said with a grimace. "You remember that merger Marzetti assured us would go through without a murmur? It's set off a regular howl."

Mac shut his eyes. "Dammit." His fingers flexed on the steering wheel and Emily saw his knuckles whiten.

"I can go," Pedro said.

Mac shook his head. "No. I was there when the proposal was made. I was the one who talked to Blankenship. He trusts me. Obviously Marzetti botched it. If we're going to pull it out, I'll have to go." He turned to Emily. "I don't want to."

She could see that in his eyes. He looked worried.

"Go where?" Tom asked from the back seat.

Mac turned to his nephew. "I've got to go to New York today."

"But you just got here!" Tom wailed. "I thought we were gonna fly that kite you brought."

Mac grimaced. "I know. I thought so, too." He reached back and tousled his nephew's hair, brown and straight, so like his own. "When I get back. And we have a sail to take. I promise."

"Will you hurry?"

Mac's eyes flickered momentarily to Emily, the heat of his gaze making her burn. "You'd better believe it. I don't intend to be gone a second longer than I have to."

"Mrs. Partridge packed for you," Pedro said. "There's a flight at four. If we leave now, we can just make it."

Mac nodded wearily. "Right." He turned to Emily. "I have to do this. It's important. I could live on my books and never look back. But the business was my father's. It's my mother's livelihood. It is——" he grimaced "—his legacy to her. She wouldn't want to live off me, so I have to keep it going for her. And Tom. It's my duty to the family."

Emily nodded. "I understand."

"I hope so," he said gravely, then leaned across and touched his lips to hers. "I hope so."

He called her from New York. Things were a bigger mess than he could have imagined. Marzetti had bananas for brains, if that. Blankenship was threatening to make trouble. He had no idea how long it would take to sort things out. Did she understand?

She did. It was probably better this way, she thought, though she didn't say so. She needed time to come to terms with the intensity of her feelings, time to adjust to thinking that something was really going to come of their relationship after all.

"I understand," she assured him.

"I'll bet," she thought she heard him mutter. But she wasn't sure, and, before she could ask, he wanted to talk to Tom.

Emily couldn't imagine how much these continual transatlantic phone calls must be costing him. He didn't seem to care. They came every day, sometimes twice. And they made both Tom and herself eager for his return.

Fiona came home. It was a joyous occasion. Everyone was there now but Mac.

Then finally one day the phone connection was better, the echo was less, and Mac said, "I'm in London."

"When're you comin' home?" Tom demanded.

"Soon," Mac promised. "And it can't be soon enough."

"And we can fly the kite?"

"Promise," Mac said.

The next day when Emily, Pedro and Tom came in from a morning ride, there was a strange silver car with a horse trailer attached parked alongside the garages and the stable. Emily saw a grin split Pedro's face the moment he saw it.

"Veronica's back!"

Veronica? But before Emily could do more than echo the name, a slender dark-haired woman appeared around the corner of the stable.

She was several years older than Emily, in her early thirties, and she wore a checked shirt and a pair of jeans that, even flecked with mud, seemed to attest to her vibrant wholesomeness. When she saw them, she waved and grinned. "Pedro! I'm home!"

"So I see." Pedro was urging them along now. "Come on. You have to meet Veronica." He slid off the horse and she put her arms around him, giving him a hug and a kiss, then stepping back to smile at him. "Handsome as ever."

Was Pedro blushing? Emily's eyes widened briefly.

But they widened even more seconds later when Veronica's gaze turned on her.

"You must be Emily," she said, still smiling, offering her hand. "I'm so glad to meet you at last. Mac's been telling me so much about you."

"*At last*"? "*Mac's been telling me so much about you*"?

Emily took Veronica's hand mindlessly, curious as to who this woman was and when she'd been talking to Mac.

Her bewilderment must have shown because Veronica laughed. "Obviously he hasn't told you anything about me. I'm Veronica Willard. I live down the lane. My late husband Geoffrey was the head of a division for Gomez International."

"I... see," Emily said, unsure what she should say.

Just then a willowy dark-haired girl of about ten came up behind Veronica, who turned and drew her forward. "And this is my daughter Lucy."

Lucy. Veronica. Emily was beginning to remember some connection at last. But Tom caught on first.

"Topper's your horse," he said eagerly to Lucy. "He's great. We went galloping this morning, me and Pedro. I love it when he gallops. He goes soooo fast."

Lucy, looking somewhat less welcoming than her mother, did manage a smile at this enthusiastic greeting. "He's pretty good," she agreed. "But you ought to see Milky Way. He's my new pony."

Tom's eyes got round as plates. "You got a new pony? Another one?"

"Uh-huh. We've been looking for just ages. Mummy said we would go to New Forest if we had to, and we did. We brought him back today. We've just put him in the stable. Want to see him?"

"You bet!" And Tom took off in Lucy's wake.

"Well," Veronica said, still smiling as she watched them go, "that must be Tom. And he likes horses, too. Lucy's positively horse crazy. I guess that means they'll be fast friends. I'm so glad. I was just going to wash. Shall we have a cup of tea?"

"Er—yes," Emily said, feeling awkward around this woman who seemed so comfortable here. Shouldn't it have been she who suggested the tea? she wondered. But Veronica was already heading toward the house.

Hurrying, Emily caught up with her. "I want to thank you for letting Tom ride your pony. I should have called before now, but no one told me and——"

"Oh, heavens, it doesn't matter. What's mine Mac can use as he pleases. He knows that. Besides, Lucy and I went up to London before we went to New Forest and he thanked me very nicely." She smiled. "A West End show and a dinner at some restaurant so trendy I don't think even the critics have discovered it yet."

"Really? How...nice." She'd thought Mac was still in New York on business until yesterday! Obviously he'd been back quite some time.

And he hadn't even bothered to come down. Why?

Because he'd rather spend time with Veronica.

The answer was so simple it smacked her right in the face. She felt suddenly ill.

"Ah, I see you found Veronica," Mrs. Partridge said to Emily as they walked into the kitchen. "Mrs. Fiona's taking a bit of a rest right now. But you go into the parlor and I'll bring the tea."

Veronica thanked her cheerfully. Emily, numb, simply followed the other woman into the parlor.

"You coming, too, Pedro?" Veronica asked.

He shook his head. "I have some work to do. Will you be joining us for dinner?"

"If I'm invited." Veronica looked at Emily.

"Of course," Pedro said before she could say anything at all.

"Then, of course, I'd be delighted." She sank down onto the sofa and smiled up at Emily. "Come sit and tell me all about yourself." She smiled. "Mac says you gave him a run for his money with Tom."

"Did he?" Emily said woodenly, sitting down before she fell.

"Now," Veronica said, still smiling, "tell me all about it."

Emily didn't think she could be drawn out, but Veronica did it. She didn't think she could like any woman who came into Mac's home and seemed to belong there, but she knew she did.

After all, she asked herself that evening as she was getting ready to go to bed that night, what was there not to like?

Veronica was charming, easy to talk to, possessed a delightful sense of humor, and further impressed Emily by her refusal to take Mac seriously.

"He tries too hard," she told Emily as they walked in the garden after dinner. "I tell him to let up."

"And does he listen?" Emily wanted to know.

Veronica shrugged. "Sometimes. But it's very deeply ingrained. He feels he has to take the world on his shoulders. All its problems, all its responsibilities."

"Yes," Emily said quietly. "I know what you mean."

"He looks out for everyone else, but never himself," Veronica said, and now she wasn't smiling. She stopped and plucked a daisy, her fingers trailing along the petals as she stared down at it. Then she lifted her gaze and her eyes met Emily's with surprising fierceness. "He deserves more. He deserves to be happy."

And Emily, stunned at the ferocity in Veronica's gaze, in her tone, could only nod.

Veronica smiled again, a sad, slightly wistful smile. "I'm glad you understand what I mean."

She understood.

She saw the easy way Mac swept Veronica up into a hug when he came home the following afternoon. Of course, Emily told herself, Veronica was in the drive when he arrived. But when Emily came out on the porch and he turned, still holding Veronica in his arms, he gave her another squeeze before he moved toward Emily.

His approach made her stiffen. She saw him frown, then proceed more slowly and give her a chaste kiss on the forehead. He started to put his arm around her. She pulled away.

For the rest of the day she witnessed the affectionate teasing between Mac and Veronica. She saw the way they raced their horses and laughed when Veronica's beat Mac's by a nose, heard the way Veronica could converse easily about Marzetti and Blankenship and listened as Mac spoke comfortably and at length about his mother's recuperation with her.

And if that wasn't enough, she became more aware than ever of his awkwardness around her. He seemed slightly aloof, distant, and his conversation with her seemed to have an almost eggshell fragility to it.

The contrast between the way he treated Veronica and the way he treated her was telling.

But if she'd held out any hope of being mistaken, Lucy resolved it the next afternoon when she and Tom were playing croquet.

They had got along rather well since lunchtime, Lucy taking her status as older and wiser seriously, making sure that Tom learned the rules and played by them. But Tom's tolerance for bossy females ran out before the game was over and he began hitting the balls randomly to irritate her.

"Stop that!" Lucy demanded. "Stop it now. That's not the way the game is played."

"I'm playin' my way," Tom said stubbornly and whacked another.

Emily, watching them from a lawn chair, debated intervening, then thought better of it.

"You can't," Lucy told him. "It's not in the rules."

"I'm making my own rules," Tom said stoutly.

"Can't!"

"Can so."

"Not!"

"Can so." He whacked another ball and Lucy snatched the mallet out of his hand.

"Hey!" Tom lunged for her and she ran. "Give it back. It's mine!"

"No. Isn't. It's Mac's."

"Yeah." Tom conceded this, still chasing her. "But he's *my* uncle."

Lucy gave a little snort, then stood her ground, hands on her hips, dark hair flying. "He might be your uncle, but he's going to be *my* dad."

Tom stopped stock-still. "He is?"

Lucy gave her head a little toss. "Of course. What do you think? He loves my mummy."

What Tom thought about that was never revealed, for at that moment Mrs. Partridge appeared in the doorway with a plateful of biscuits and glasses of milk.

"Time for a little break?" she suggested.

Argument forgotten, Tom and Lucy went running.

Emily, having had it spelled out for her, didn't move.

Of course it all made sense.

They were perfect for each other—Mac and Veronica. Mac in his mid-thirties, Veronica just a year or two younger. Both talented and well-educated, both from the same background, with the same interests, the same desires. Emily was an American, eight years younger, less educated, less sophisticated, less of everything.

So why was he marrying Emily? Duty. Responsibility.

Emily might love him in spite of him, in spite of herself. She might marry him for that love. But love alone wouldn't make Mac marry. Duty would. So he would marry her and love Veronica.

No!

No, Emily thought desperately. Not again!

It was like Marc and Lisette all over again—not that Marc would have ever married for something as altruistic as duty, but the fact was that neither he nor Mac loved her. Each of them loved someone else.

Veronica was hardly the classic "other woman." She wasn't bitchy in the least. Nor was she mean to Emily. The only things she had said were oblique. She had hinted that Mac shouldn't marry for duty alone. But she hadn't stood in his way. She wouldn't.

But would she be there for Mac even when he was married to Emily? It didn't bear thinking about!

That night, alone in her luxurious bed, Emily knew that marrying Mac didn't bear thinking about, either. Dreams were just that—dreams. Fantasies and nothing more. Reality was that he loved a woman much more suitable than she was. Reality was that marrying her was his way of taking care of her, of Tom, of his mother. Reality was that, in asking her to marry him, Mac was doing what he did best: assuming responsibility for everyone else at his own expense.

No, she couldn't marry him.

It had been risky enough to contemplate when she'd thought that, despite their bad start, they might make a go of it, that there was a faint chance that he might come to love her. Now she knew better. He loved Veronica. And he would make them all miserable by marrying Emily—unless she stopped him! She had to leave. It was only what she'd planned from the first. But if her original decision was the same, Tom wasn't.

In a matter of a few weeks he had become devoted to his grandmother. He adored Mac, who had taken the place of a father to him. He liked being with Pedro, but his devotion was saved for his uncle. Most of his sentences these days began "Uncle Mac this' and "Uncle

Mac that." He tagged after Mac whenever his uncle was home.

He had settled into the neighborhood as well. The gardener let him help him with the plantings, the stable boy let him curry the ponies. Mrs. Partridge gave him treats whenever he passed through the kitchen. In Eric he had found a best friend, and Eric's family had practically adopted him as their own.

Yesterday Veronica had given him a riding lesson. And within hours he'd been her devoted slave as well. If there was anyone with whom he didn't maintain total rapport, it was Lucy. They squabbled with frequency. But Emily remembered squabbles with her own brother. She also remembered how much she loved and missed him still.

Just an hour ago Tom had sat on the edge of his bed and dug his toe into the rug before looking up at her with his wide eyes. "Eric's lucky," he told her.

Emily dropped his shirt and jeans in the laundry basket. "Oh. Why is that?"

"He's got a brother and a sister. I wish I had a brother or a sister."

Would he want Lucy for a sister? Emily wondered now. What about other children Mac and Veronica might have?

The thought sent a short sharp stab of pain to her heart. She had to leave. She had no choice.

But take Tom? She wished the decision were as simple as it had once been. But the life she was going to in the States would be far from settled.

She wanted to go back to university, study English, learn how to teach it as a second language. It would take hard work and long hours. She had money to see her through, but she wouldn't be able to give Tom the sort of life she would want him to have. Not for several years. Before she knew the Gomez family, she'd been sure that whatever living arrangements she came up with would be preferable to the loveless, bitter environment she was certain they would provide.

Now she knew that wasn't true. She wished Tom were ready to leave, too, then hated herself for wanting him to be as unhappy as she was.

For the first time in months, she could see that Tom was happy. He went to bed singing. He woke up smiling. He was comfortable, well-adjusted, loved. He had a life again. The sort of life David and Mari would have wanted for him. The only thing that didn't fit in his life was his aunt.

And, realizing that, Emily knew what she had to do.

She waited until the following afternoon when Fiona was napping and Mac and Pedro had to go into London for a business meeting. She chatted amiably with Mrs. Partridge about the dinner menu, listened to the groom telling her how well Master Tom was doing with his riding, walked one last time through the daisies that lined the garden. Then she packed her bags, wrote Mac a terse farewell note, called a taxi and left.

One thing she didn't do: she didn't take Tom.

CHAPTER TEN

TOM had understood.

Emily never would have left if she'd felt he hadn't, if he'd felt she was abandoning him. But before she called the taxi she had taken him upstairs and sat him down to explain. She had been determined that she wouldn't cry. If she did, she knew he would never believe her reason for going.

She had laid it out logically, telling him that she loved him, would always love him, but that she had to go, that there was no work for her here.

"What about me? Taking care of me?" he'd demanded with childish innocence.

And Emily, heart breaking, had assured him that his Uncle Mac and his grandma would take very good care of him.

"But I want you. I want you to stay and marry Mac and be my second mom."

"I'd love to be your second mom," Emily said gently, "but it's not that simple. Married people have to love each other."

"Don't you love Uncle Mac?"

"That's not the point," she said desperately. "He doesn't love me."

"Course he does," Tom said, as if he couldn't imagine anyone who wouldn't.

Emily shook her head. "No."

Tom scowled.

"It'll be all right," she assured him. "Believe me. I'll write. And...and I'll come visit when I can," she promised, hoping instead that Mac would, out of mercy, send him to see her.

"But..." Tom's lower lip quivered. Emily's own was none too stiff, but she swallowed the lump in her throat, willed down the tears in her eyes, and bent to hug him close.

"I love you, darling. Do you believe that?"

Eyes downcast, Tom nodded. "Can't I come with you?"

Emily fought the temptation. Yes, she wanted to say. Oh, yes. Yes! But she shook her head. "You wouldn't be happy, love. I'll have to get a little bitsy apartment somewhere while I go to school. You wouldn't have a garden to play in or Eric right down the road. You wouldn't have Topper or Grandma or...or Uncle Mac."

"I'd have you," Tom said stubbornly.

"You'll always have me," Emily said. "I promise." She lifted his chin so that he looked into her eyes. His own were bright with unshed tears. His mulish expression was so like Mac's that her own eyes misted and threatened to betray her. "I love you, Tommy. I always will, no matter where I am. Understand?"

He nodded solemnly, then threw his arms around her and hugged her tight. Emily hugged him back, memorizing the sturdy solid feel of him, the soft hair that brushed her cheek, the fierce grip of his hands. And then she loosed his hold on her and stepped back, smiling crookedly down at him.

"You take good care of your grandmother."

"I will," he promised.

"And be a good boy."

"I am," he said indignantly.

She nodded, blinking back her tears, still smiling. "I know you are."

At that moment the taxi appeared, coming slowly up the drive, and Emily bent to give Tom one last swift kiss. Then she put her note for Mac on the table in the library, picked up her bag and headed out the door.

She had waved until the taxi drove around the curve. Then, resolutely, she faced forward and didn't look back.

It had been a week now, and she hadn't looked back yet.

She had ridden the length and breadth of England for the first three days, taking trains indiscriminately, uncaring, trying simply to stop crying, trying to come to terms with what she'd done.

She'd known she should stop, get some rest, get herself together. But she couldn't wish herself on anyone in the state she was when she'd left Tom behind. But finally aimlessness wasn't enough. She had to get on with her life, focus on the future, go on from here.

She'd considered going to the States at once, then rejected it for the time being. When she got there she wouldn't have a place to stay, wouldn't have a job to go to. Going back to college would take some arranging. Arranging was beyond her right now.

She had called the Evanses from a little Scottish town on the North Sea. "Could I stop in for a few days?" she'd asked Sian. "To regroup. I—I need to think things out."

And Sian, as welcoming and supportive as Howell had ever been, didn't even say, More man trouble? She'd just said, "By all means, come."

Howell, home on a two-week holiday, had met her at the station and bundled her into his Jaguar and drove her home. He asked no questions. Nor did Sian. Probably they didn't need to, Emily thought. Howell made his living studying faces; Sian made hers sculpting them. They'd only have had to look at hers to know her pain.

They'd simply given her time and space to come to terms with it, to face the future on her own.

She'd been cosseted, cared for and comforted in almost silent solicitude for the past four days now. She'd spent hour upon hour walking the shingle beach, following the seawall out to the point, and tramping the hillside trails among the sheep that grazed near their windswept Welsh home.

In between times, the Evanses had fed her good food, played her soft music, and given her good books. Sian had even got her working with clay.

"It's good for you," she'd said as she handed the first slab to Emily. "Soothing. Gives you something to work your pain out on."

Emily couldn't deny she needed to do that. And the feel of the soft, smooth clay under her fingers did seem to have a therapeutic effect. After that, every time she'd wanted to reach for the phone to call Tom, she'd reached for the clay instead.

She'd written to him, just as she'd promised. She didn't say where she was.

Not that it would matter, she thought. Certainly Tom wouldn't be able to come looking for her, and, given his freedom, she was sure that Mac would only be grateful.

He had what he wanted. Both Tom and Veronica. He wouldn't bother.

Eventually she'd talked about going back to college with Sian. She'd explored possibilities of a life beyond modeling with Howell. She never talked about Mac at all.

When she'd finally decided they needed some sort of explanation for her appearance, she'd told them simply that she had just come from leaving Tom with his mother's family.

"It was the right thing to do," she'd said, and known it was true. "He'll be happiest there. But it's hard. I miss him," she'd told them finally that afternoon at tea. "I miss him a lot."

If either Howell or Sian suspected that there was more to it than that, they didn't say. Sian just put another cup of hot tea into her hands, and Howell gave her a hug.

"Go and walk out on the point," Howell advised her. "Life will look better from there."

Emily went.

It was early evening and the sun was just beginning to set out over the ocean. The wind whipped through her hair, the clouds scudded along overhead. Every day she walked here, spent hours contemplating the ever-changing sea. She found it as soothing as the clay, maybe more so. The clay she could control; the ocean she could not.

Like life.

There were things she could control, direct, mold, and others that she had no power over.

Like Mac.

It was the first time she had deliberately thought about him since she'd left.

Until now, every time his name had come into her head, every time his face had appeared in her mind, she'd banished them. It was too painful to remember her hopes, her dreams, her silly flights of fantasy, too hard to face what a fool she'd been. Some women just picked the wrong men, she'd heard. She must be one of them.

She stopped at the point and hung out over the edge, leaning against the railing, looking at the waves that crashed far below. This height didn't bother her the way the height had in Chamonix. Instead it tempted her. She leaned over, relishing the dizzy feel it gave her, preferring it to the hollow anguish she had been feeling.

"Emmmileee!"

The sound was faint at first, carried the other way by the wind and Emily wasn't even sure she heard it. She glanced back up the path, saw Howell in his navy anorak, far up the hill, heading toward her. She waved and turned away again, then swung herself up onto the railing to sit and watch the ship, far out, heading into the sun.

"Emmmileee!" It came again, louder now. It sounded frantic. Angry almost. She frowned. Howell was only angry when the lighting was wrong or the models had zits or his assistant loaded the wrong film.

She turned, curious now.

It wasn't Howell at all.

It was Mac, sliding down the path, almost running now, his hair whipping in the wind, his shoes skidding on the rough gravel as he came.

Emily scrambled down off the rail, then backed against it, wishing desperately for a way out, trapped by the knowledge that, save jumping, there wasn't one.

He jerked to a stop in front of her, grabbing her into his arms. "What in bloody hell do you think you're doing, jumping like that?"

"J-ump?" Her voice barely worked.

"You flaming idiot! Haven't you got an ounce of sense? Don't you know what it would do to Tom? To me?"

Emily stared at him, cleared her throat, tried again. "Jump?" Yes, it was working now. It sounded incredulous. She *was* incredulous. "Are you crazy? I wasn't going to jump! I was watching the sunset!"

His hands fell back and his face suffused with color. She saw a pulse ticking wildly in his throat. He looked at her, at the sky, at the ground.

"Oh," he muttered at last. He stuffed his hands into the pockets of what was in fact, Emily noted, Howell's anorak. She shifted her gaze to his face. He looked awful. His eyes were bloodshot and underscored with dark smudges. His face was drawn, his forehead furrowed. She wondered what deal had fallen through now.

Besides her.

Surely he hadn't come after her?

Her anger flared at the thought. She'd given him what he wanted, dammit! Was he going to put duty above everything? Lord, she hoped not. She couldn't keep fighting him off! A woman only had so much willpower.

She looked at him belligerently. "What are you doing here?"

"Why the hell do you think I'm here. You left!"

"I left a note."

"Yeah. 'Dear Mac, I can't marry you. It would be all wrong.' What the hell is that supposed to mean?"

"Just what I said. It wouldn't work!"

"Why not?"

"It just wouldn't."

"Explain to me."

She shook her head.

"You just...changed your mind?" His tone was bitter, his gaze ironic.

Emily clenched her teeth briefly. "Yes, I changed my mind. What do you care? You got what you wanted, didn't you?"

He just stared at her. Behind them waves crashed. Overhead a gull battled the wind. Emily lifted her chin defiantly.

Slowly Mac shook his head. "No," he said quietly. "No, I didn't."

It was Emily's turn to stare, taken aback by what sounded like quiet desperation. "No, perhaps not," she said angrily after a moment. "Not completely, anyway. Perhaps you'd have preferred a built-in nanny for a wife as long as you could get your love somewhere else!"

"What!"

"You don't love me. You want to marry me because of Tom. Because I'm his aunt and it will make him happy."

"Is that *really* what you think? When I made love to you was I making love to Tom's auntie, Emily? When I asked you to marry me was I asking Tom's auntie?" His voice rose against the wind. His eyes were glittering, the skin across his cheekbones drew taut.

Emily, not wanting to remember the loving, not wanting any recollection of the passion consummated between them that night in Chamonix, looked away. "What else?" she said scornfully. "We come from completely different worlds. We have different backgrounds. We want very different things!"

She wished he would go away. She wished he wouldn't talk about when he'd made love to her. She held herself rigid, refusing to shiver though his touch made her burn and the wind made her cold. She stared straight out to sea, unblinking.

She heard him sigh and saw him bend his head. His fingers gradually lost their grip on her arms, slid down the length of her sleeves, lingered a moment on her hands, then fell limply to his sides. The fire was gone in his eyes now, the flame of his anger burnt out.

He looked infinitely weary and pained. His shoulders slumped, his fingers flexed and clenched against his thighs. He shut his eyes.

"It's all gone wrong, hasn't it?" he said. "Right from the very start. Why should I have imagined it would change now?"

He opened his eyes and looked at her dispiritedly, then fished in the pocket of Howell's jacket and brought out an envelope.

"This is for you." He handed it to her. "Tom's at the house waiting for you," he said, and turned and began to walk away.

Emily stared after him, her fingers fumbling with the envelope, her mind groping to make sense of his words.

Tom? At the house? Here?

At last she got the envelope open. Numbly she pulled out a very official-looking document, signed and witnessed, stamped and sealed. Her eyes scanned down it. She bit her lip.

Alejandro Tomás Gomez y MacPherson and Fiona Elizabeth MacPherson de Gomez hereby relinquished any and all claim to Thomas David Musgrave, a minor, now and until his majority. They acknowledged that he would remain in the custody and under the guardianship of Emily Frances Musgrave...

Emily's eyes blurred. Her hands shook. She looked up frantically to find Mac climbing slowly, his head bent.

"Mac!" She was running before she could stop herself. "Mac! Wait!"

He stopped, but he didn't turn. He waited, but he didn't look at her.

She reached him, caught his sleeve, pulled him around. "Why?" she demanded. "Why?"

Fleetingly his eyes met hers. "Because he's yours," he said hoarsely. "Because he belongs with you."

"But your mother——"

"Understands. I...explained to her. I told her everything. About not telling you who I was, about trying to manipulate you." His mouth twisted. "She thinks I behaved like an idiot." There was a hectic line of color running along his cheekbones. "She's right."

"You...you did what you thought was right. At first, anyway." From somewhere Emily found the courage to allow him that.

His mouth twisted. "I had no excuse. Not really. She wanted me to find you, to see if you'd bring Tom for a visit, maybe help you out. I wanted more than that. I'd heard rumors—about you...and Evans. I got on my high horse. I'd decided without even knowing you that you were not the sort of person who ought to be Tom's guardian. I never stopped to think I'd make a worse one, that I had far less right to him than you did, that the Gomezes had forfeited any rights they might have had long ago." His jaw tightened, and Emily saw him swallow hard.

"You missed your sister."

He nodded. "More than you can imagine. It was wrong, what my father wanted her to do. I could see that even when I was being his right-hand man and trying to get her to do it. But I'd been brought up to do what I was told. If it was for the good of the family, you did it. No excuse, again, but I'd never been in love. I didn't understand. Then."

Until Veronica, she thought, and her heart ached.

"I'm sorry, Em," he went on gruffly, "for what I did to them. For everything I did to you. I wish I could have said it to your brother, to Mari. The only thing I can do is say it to you, and try to make it up to Tom." He looked away, across toward the horizon, blinking against the fierce red of the sun.

"I...thank you," she murmured at last.

His mouth twisted grimly. "You're welcome." He turned and started up the path again.

"I'm not going to take him, though," she said to his back.

His head swiveled to look at her. "Why not?"

"He's happy with you. He has a home, a grandmother, an uncle. He'll——" she swallowed, then forced herself to go on "—have a mother, a sister, maybe new siblings." She tried to smile.

Mac was staring at her. "What are you talking about?"

"You. Getting married."

"I'm not getting married," he said harshly. "Not if you aren't marrying me."

"But that's ridiculous," Emily argued. "Duty isn't everything! If you love her, you must!"

Mac frowned. "Love who?"

Emily rolled her eyes. "Veronica."

"Veronica? You think I love Veronica?"

"She said——"

"She couldn't have said I loved her!"

"No, but——" Emily shook her head "—she said you do everything out of duty. She said you always look out for everyone else but never yourself. She said you deserved more."

"I didn't ask you to marry me out of duty. Ever."

"But..." Emily's voice faded. She looked at him closely, took in again the desperation in his eyes, the taut sternness of his mouth.

"You hugged her," she said lamely, "when you came back."

Mac gave her an exasperated look. "She was standing in the driveway. She's my friend. And I would have hugged you in an instant, but you didn't look as if you wanted me to touch you. I was afraid to. Things were too fragile."

Emily remembered her suspicions, remembered how she had stiffened when he'd come toward her. She looked at him more closely, saw the need in him.

Yes, Emily thought. Oh, yes. She felt a faint flickering of hope and wondered if she was a fool for feeling it.

"Lucy said you were going to be her dad," she told him softly.

He didn't seem surprised. "Lucy wants a dad. Her own died four years ago. For the last two she's had her sights set on me. I'll never come through, but I think Pedro might come up to scratch eventually."

"Pedro?"

"He's a slow worker. Not a 'fools rush in' type, like yours truly," Mac said wryly. "But I think he may make a move one day."

"Not you?" Emily said now, her voice still faint, but getting stronger.

"Never me. For me it was always you."

Emily stared.

"I didn't ask you to marry me because you were Tom's aunt," Mac went on firmly.

"Then why——?"

"Oh, hell, why do you think? I've told you often enough! I loved you. Love you," he corrected harshly. "For all the good it's done me." He twisted away, starting up the hill again. Emily stared after him, stunned, trying to adjust, to believe.

"Mac, wait!"

For a moment she thought he wasn't going to stop. But then he did, turning back slowly to face her.

"I didn't realize," she said softly, moving towards him. "I hoped, but I didn't believe."

He took a step backward, staring at her. "What do you mean?" His voice was hoarse. He was looking at her with every bit as much trepidation as she had felt facing him. It gave her the courage to tell the truth.

"I mean I love you, too."

He went stock-still. Behind them the waves crashed against the rocks. Gulls wheeled and dived overhead. From somewhere far away she could hear the plaintive bleat of the sheep.

"Emily?" There was a world of doubt and a hint of hope in his voice. "Don't say it just to torment me. Don't say it unless you mean it. Please!"

She came to him, touched his arm, smiled again, nodding. "I mean it. I do."

He shook his head. "In spite of everything?" His voice was ragged. His hands gripped her arms.

Emily lay her hand against his cheek. "In spite of... because of... I don't know precisely which," she admitted. "I only know I love you because... because you're you."

He let out a sound somewhere between a moan and a laugh. "Oh, Lord, Emily. I don't believe it. I don't deserve it!"

"Well, no, you don't," Emily agreed frankly, managing a shaky laugh as he hauled her hard against him.

"It isn't funny," he muttered. And then he was kissing her desperately, passionately, with every ounce of need that he had in him. And Emily was kissing him, too.

It was like being brought back to life after an eternity of death. It was like nourishment for the soul. Her heart overflowed.

"I thought I'd driven you off forever," he muttered at last, when his lips lifted from hers. "I knew I'd hurt you in the first place, in Chamonix when you found out who I was. So I was trying to play it cool, give you time to recover, give you time—I hoped—to figure out that you still loved me. I thought I'd done it. And when I came back from London and found out you'd gone——" His voice broke and he shook his head.

She put her arms around him again, kissing him tenderly, reveling in his strength, in his hunger, in the fierce hard hammering of his heart. "I couldn't stay," she told him. "Not when I thought you loved Veronica. Not when I thought we didn't have a chance."

He pulled back and looked down into her eyes. "Do we have a chance, Emily?"

And she touched her lips to his. "Yes," she whispered. "Oh, yes."

"Thank God," Mac murmured and lay his cheek against hers.

Emily snuggled against him, locking her hands behind his back, absorbing the warmth of his body, the joy of his presence, the knowledge that it was hers to share.

"How did you find me?" she asked him finally.

"I almost didn't. I called that friend of yours in Barcelona first."

"Gloria?"

"Yeah. But she wouldn't tell me anything. Like a stone wall, that woman."

"I made her promise before I left."

"Yeah, well, she carried it out to the letter," Mac said drily. "So then I went to Tom's school. Talked to some guy called Duggan who said he wanted to marry you."

"You talked to Bob?"

"For all the good it did me," he growled. "But you're damned well not going to marry him!"

"I don't want to," Emily said softly.

"Good." He kissed her hard. "Then I tried to track down Evans." He grimaced. "That took a while. He was supposedly in Greece. But he'd just left by the time I got through to the hotel there. And it took me another two days to get someone to give me his private number.

All I could get from his damned secretary was that he was on holiday and she wasn't at liberty to say where."

His fierce expression made Emily smile.

"When your letter came, the postmark was Wales. I knew you had to be at his place then, so I went down to London and took the old witch on in her own office. She gave it to me," he added with considerable satisfaction.

"You went to a lot of trouble," Emily said, which was something of an understatement. She was looking at him, awed, wondering why she'd ever in the first place thought she could escape this man if he put his mind to finding her.

"I had to," Mac said simply. "I had really pretty much given up on making you love me by then. But I had to see you, to give you the papers. I wanted you to know that I'd stopped trying to do things my way. I was just going to give them to you and leave." He shrugged, flushing. "Then I thought I saw you trying to do away with yourself and I lost my head. I don't want to lose you, Emily."

"You haven't lost me," Emily said, letting her lips brush his jawline. "You never will."

"Promise?" His eyes were dark and unreadable.

Emily's hand touched his cheek. "Oh, yes."

He kissed her again, then. And his kiss was a promise, too, one that invoked the love they'd shared in Chamonix and the fulfillment they'd found there in each other's arms.

Finally Mac pulled back, breathing hard. "We'd better get up to the house," he said roughly. "They'll be wondering what's going on. Your Howell doesn't much trust me."

Emily cocked her head. "No? What makes you say that?"

Mac grimaced. "The way he looked at me. The questions he asked. Wanted to know if I was the reason you were moping around looking as if you'd just been run over by a truck."

"Did you tell him you were?"

"I didn't know, did I?" Mac said gruffly. "I was afraid it was just that you were missing Tom—and hating me."

"No. I was loving you, and hating myself for being such a fool."

"I've never loved anyone else in my life the way I love you," he told her as he looped an arm around her waist and hugged her against him. They began to walk up the path. "When will you marry me?"

"Today. Tomorrow. As soon as you like."

He grinned. "That's the first amenable thing you've said to me since we've met."

Emily nudged him with her elbow. "Oh, I can think of one or two others."

"Maybe," he conceded and dropped a kiss on her forehead.

"Shall we live in England with your mother?"

"If you want. Or Madrid. Or Chamonix."

"Or Singapore," Emily added dryly.

"Even Singapore," Mac said equably. "Wherever you're happiest."

"I'm happiest with you," Emily told him, "wherever you are, whether you're in England or Spain doing business or traveling and doing research. We liked doing research," she added a little shyly.

He looked faintly embarrassed. "I can't lie to you any more, Em. What we were doing... that wasn't exactly intended to be a research jaunt. Not for a book, anyway."

"No? What were you researching?" Emily asked archly.

He gave her a self-conscious grin. "Er—you."

She shot him a hard look.

"I wanted to know you. And the more I knew, the more I wanted to know. And finally I found out the most important thing of all. I found out I love you."

They reached the front steps of the Evanses' house now and saw Tom beaming at them and waving from the lighted window.

Mac gave him a brief thumbs-up sign, then turned and drew Emily into his arms, kissing her with a thoroughness that left Tom and the Evanses in no doubt about the outcome of their conversation.

"I love you, too, Alejandro Gomez y MacPherson," Emily said against his lips. "And I will for the rest of my life."

MILLION DOLLAR SWEEPSTAKES (III)

No purchase necessary. To enter the sweepstakes and receive the Free Books and Surprise Gift, follow the directions published and complete and mail your "Win A Fortune" Game Card. If not taking advantage of the book and gift offer or if the "Win A Fortune" Game Card is missing, you may enter by hand-printing your name and address on a 3" X 5" card and mailing it (limit: one entry per envelope) via First Class Mail to: Million Dollar Sweepstakes (III) "Win A Fortune" Game, P.O. Box 1867, Buffalo, NY 14269-1867, or Million Dollar Sweepstakes (III) "Win A Fortune" Game, P.O. Box 609, Fort Erie, Ontario L2A 5X3. When your entry is received, you will be assigned sweepstakes numbers. To be eligible entries must be received no later than March 31, 1996. No liability is assumed for printing errors or lost, late or misdirected entries. Odds of winning are determined by the number of eligible entries distributed and received.

Sweepstakes open to residents of the U.S. (except Puerto Rico), Canada, Europe and Taiwan who are 18 years of age or older. All applicable laws and regulations apply. Sweepstakes offer void wherever prohibited by law. Values of all prizes are in U.S. currency. This sweepstakes is presented by Torstar Corp, its subsidiaries and affiliates, in conjunction with book, merchandise and/or product offerings. For a copy of the official rules governing this sweepstakes offer, send a self-addressed, stamped envelope (WA residents need not affix return postage) to: MILLION DOLLAR SWEEPSTAKES (III) Rules, P.O. Box 4573, Blair, NE 68009, USA.

SWP-H994

MIRA
TM